*A
Harlequin
Romance*

OTHER
Harlequin Romances
by MARGARET WAY

Many of these titles are available at your local bookseller,
or through the Harlequin Reader Service.

For a free catalogue listing all available Harlequin Romances,
send your name and address to:

HARLEQUIN READER SERVICE,
M.P.O. Box 707, Niagara Falls, N.Y. 14302
Canadian address: Stratford, Ontario, Canada.

or use order coupon at back of book.

RETURN
TO BELLE AMBER

by

MARGARET WAY

HARLEQUIN BOOKS   TORONTO
WINNIPEG

Original hard cover edition published in 1971
by Mills & Boon Limited.

© Margaret Way 1971

SBN 373-01840-1

Harlequin edition published December, 1974

The Harlequin trade mark, consisting of the word
HARLEQUIN and the portrayal of a Harlequin, is registered
in the United States Patent Office and in the Canada Trade
Marks Office.

Printed in Canada

CHAPTER I

THE gold was fading from the sky. It was turning imperceptibly to a delicate green, like cool, running water. A capering wind whipped up with the dusk skeining her long black hair across her face and throat. Karen roused herself from a world of random little thoughts and hurried on home. Soon it would be dark and Philip would be waiting. She turned up the collar of her coat, her long slim legs flashing, her heels on the pavement tapping out the same urgent message: Philip will be waiting: Philip will be waiting.

In her own quiet cul-de-sac the roar of the traffic, the relentless procession of cars, buses and darting taxi-cabs was suddenly obliterated. The fine old houses stood in a world of their own; a world of silence and gentle stability. The winter-into-spring blend of atmosphere was brisk and invigorating and in every garden the wattles were bursting into fluffy gold blossom. The sight and scent of them prodded her memory and induced a bitter-sweet nostalgia, a fragrant reminder of days long past. Karen gave an involuntary gasp, for an instant suspended in time.

In front of the old wine cellar stood a magnificent acacia. With each spring it burst into dazzling blossom: masses upon masses of softest yellow constellations that swayed against the whitewashed stone building. A very long time before someone had built a circular bench around its broad base, and there the children loved to congregate, in plain sight and scent of the mysterious and wonderfully spooky old place — the cellar. It was haunted, of course, by old Matthew Amber, who had built it and stocked it and loved it and gone there to die. How many childish fantasies had they woven around him — the tall spectral figure that roamed the gloomy underground tunnels stacked

5

high with dusty old bottles bottles that glowed ruby and ane-
thyst when rubbed off and held up to the light.

At the back of the cellar was a squat stone wall trailing ivy
with a background of camellias and low-growing azaleas, and
beyond that the glasshouses crammed to the ceiling with exotic
plants from all over the world. Aunt Patricia favoured orchids
and was the possessor of an enviable "green finger". As soon
as the temperature dropped a few degrees she would rush off
to the greenhouse to check the humidity for her beloved
cattleyas, for once the orchids budded they would bloom on for
weeks at a time.

One lovely image after another flashed across Karen's mind
like slides on a projection screen. Faster and faster they flew,
absorbing her entire attention. At the foot of the embankment,
approaching the vineyards, was a small pond guarded by wil-
lows, where fish liked to dart, leaving flashes of silver and gold.
Rikki got spanked once for trying to fish there. Rikki was always the rebel, a small boy with silver-gilt hair!

The breeze tugged at her hair, pulling her out of it. Karen
blinked her eyes fiercely. It all seemed a million years ago, anyway. The golden days of Belle Amber! The days of her childhood; the halcyon days that could never be recaptured.

Nearing her own front gate, great ferny fronds groped
through the fence towards her and caught at her coat. Karen
bent down and broke off a few with her hand. Despite all her
efforts the garden was getting too much for her. She could cope
with the lawns, but the long-established flower beds were beyond her. She shifted her gaze to the rambling old house, almost a mansion. A light shone dimly through the living room
curtains. The house was getting too much for her. It was too
big, too lonely, but at least it was hers. She had high rates but
no rent to worry about. Even so, the next few years would be a
battle to make ends meet. She braced her slender shoulders,
warding off a sudden burst of depression. She was tired, that
was it. Wednesday was always a long tiring day with a straight

6

un of dull pupils and theory classes after school. Responsibili-
ties always seemed more overwhelming when one was tired.
Characteristically she began to hum quietly under her breath,
fighting off the plague of doubts and self-recriminations that
seemed to close in with the dusk.

The front door of the house opened and a boy of about ten
careered down the stairs. Karen's face changed as she watched
his swift flight, and an imperturbable gaiety spread over her
lovely mouth. Philip was a handsome child with dark hair and
dark eyes, his skin a clear olive. She dropped her music case
and heavy shopping bag prepared for the high-spirited launch
he made at her.

"Karo! Karo, guess what? I've busted my knee again, would
you believe it?"

His sister looked down at him, the lovely gaiety still on her
mouth. "I would, and you'll survive, my pet. Did you put any
disinfectant on it?"

Philip nodded his head matter-of-factly. "Sure. But you
should see the dents in the bike. I don't know how I'll ever get
them out."

Karen clicked her tongue in commiseration and the two of
them walked up the steps, flanked by stone jars overflowing
with massed *Alba Magna* azaleas. Their arms were entwined,
their dark heads together. They were very close. It had always
been so. Even before their mother had died Karen had been
everything to her small brother – mother, sister, brother, con-
fidante. Eva Hartmann had spent the last eight years of her life
mysteriously an invalid, a strange and bitter woman with an
impenetrable protective veneer, aloof from her own children,
obsessed with the past, obsessed with the Ambers, her own
wealthy clan and the family who had contrived in so many
ways to ruin her husband.

As a very young girl Karen had suffered recurrent night-
mares from her mother's tales of Amber misdeeds and machin-
ations. The expression on that once beautiful face still disturbed

7

her dreams; the expression Karen came later to recognise as a deep and implacable hatred.

One of the few legacies Karen had of the past eight years was a courageous independence of thought and spirit, an aspect of her character that was fostered by nature, and strengthened by the events and environment of her life.

Inside the house the hall light was blazing. The letter was there again! Karen picked it up carefully, her hands trembling. She glanced down at Philip.

"Go and wash your hands and set the table for tea."

He looked at her patiently, his dark eyes alerted. "I've already done that, Karo. What's in the letter?" He searched his sister's pale face. Her skin gleamed opalescent under the bright light.

"Start on your homework, then," she murmured abstractedly, her eyes already on the typewritten page, the huge cheque that accompanied it. She separated them uneasily while Philip went off, unprotesting without trying to divert or offer comfort. He was already something of a philosopher. Karen was worried. He could always read the signs, but she was not prone to airing her worries. He would start on his homework. Besides every term he seemed to get more of it.

His sister walked into the living room, gazing down at the letter. The house seemed very still around her, almost as though it were listening. So they wanted them. The almighty Ambers! Her eyes moved down the page to the black forceful signature, as distinctive and vigorous as its well-remembered owner – GUY AMBER.

Lessons painfully learnt are forever remembered! Karen lifted her dark head, her great tawny eyes flashing like topazes in the light. No wonder her mother had hated him. What an insufferable style he had, though the technique was flawless, almost surgical in its clean sweeping thrusts. She could almost applaud his easy, positive assumption that she would fall in with his wishes. Her soft mouth held a sobering maturity. No, not wishes, precisely – commands. That was it. Commands,

8

and he was a man long used to giving them.

So the great Guy Amber had come forward to look after the orphans. Eight long years later he would look after the orphans. He would take care of Pip's education. Philip was, after all, an Amber. He would go into the family business. Perhaps take his father's place . . . never!

The thoughts in her mind were clear, clear and cold and precise. Karen screwed up the sheet of paper with a single convulsive movement and pitched it into the fireplace with stunning accuracy, her young, almost breakable body taut with fiery disdain.

She would look after Philip. She always would, for as long as he needed her. She was nineteen, not ninety, and she was earning a good salary – her Conservatorium diploma saw to that. She was already assistant music mistress at St. Hilda's, the exclusive girls' school where she was once a pupil. All those years of study had paid off.

Her mother had kept her hard at it, though she derived no great pleasure from her daughter's accomplishment – "A necessary investment" – Eva Hartmann had called it as she paid out the high fees. Karen's undeniable gift, an inheritance from her father, had done the rest. Karen's eyes swung round the living room, fixing details. It was a beautiful room really, faded but still beautiful. A woman's room, highly individual, with each piece carefully selected by her mother. It still held her essence. There was no lingering trace of their dear dead father, no element of masculine intrusion, save the piano. Only the piano remained to remind the children of their father. Stephen Hartmann had been a highly gifted pianist. The piano, a six-foot concert grand, had been his own cherished possession.

The French Impressionist paintings that shimmered from the walls were her mother's favourites and over the piano hung a fine Dégas print, so deeply familiar to her from long hours of staring at it, the little dancing girl's tutu caught in a halo of light. Even the books were her mother's – a whole wall of them,

9

beautifully jacketed, with separate niches for display pieces of porcelain and china, crystal and ivory, coloured glass objects that winked in the light.

Karen's eyes came back to the piano, open as usual, her music scattered helter-skelter all over the top from the morning's frantic search for a Debussy *Arabesque*. How often in the past when she practised had she looked up to find her mother's eyes fixed on her ... on the piano; seeing and unseeing, her expression fixed, her fine dark eyes clouded with remembrances.

Ever sensitive to her mother's moods, Karen had only once broached the subject of her father. Then her mother's taut answer, the queer tone she had used, made Karen forever back away from the subject: "We won't speak of your father, Karen. For me, at least, it's a kind of peace without him."

Karen had never forgotten it – had she allowed herself to dwell on it, never forgiven it. Her father had been very dear to her. She was, after all, made in his image. To have lived all her life so close to her mother and then to discover in one painful instant that she really didn't know her at all came as a shattering realisation, part of the disillusionment of growing up. Something dreadful had happened to Eva Hartmann, but when or how it had happened Karen had been too young to tell. It was impossible to pinpoint the exact period of time, though she had gone over and over it.

One thing was certain, the Ambers were up to their necks in it. On their shoulders lay a great measure of the blame for Eva Hartmann's disenchantment, the great ache that gnawed away her fragile bones. Only with approaching maturity did Karen come to glimpse the exquisite pleasure her mother derived from her suffering, the implacable bitterness she wore like a shield. Her death was a shock, complete and absolute, but after the first rush of grief came a sense of release, a lightening of the burden that Eva Hartmann had knowingly or unknowingly conferred on her children.

Abruptly, Karen came out of her reverie. She hurried out of the room and ran up the stairs to her bedroom. The white bobbles on the high canopy danced as she threw her coat down on the bed. She pulled her dress over her head and reached into the wardrobe for her slacks and a sweater. It would only take ten minutes to heat the casserole through. She was a clever and capable young woman, but she thought little of her own varied talents. She hadn't the time. The days and nights spun by endlessly, none of them free from some form of anxiety.

Inevitably, her eye fell on an early framed portrait of her mother and father, and she checked in her stride to look down at it. Two handsome young people gazed back at her; her mother looking directly at the camera, her face, despite the outdated hairstyle, striking, imperious even; her father looking slightly past the camera, both of them caught at a high point in their lives, eyes and mouth smiling, happy and confident, facing the future with the assured arrogance of the young and secure. And they had been secure – then.

Her father's family, the Hartmanns, had been among the colony's earliest pioneers of the vine with a small but excellent vineyard and winery, and her mother's family – the Ambers, then a big wine-making firm, now controlled twenty of the finest vineyards in three States and a great trading company.

A merger between the two families had been inevitable. The Hartmann vineyards adjoined the Amber estates. It was only a matter of time before they swallowed them up. Stephen Hartmann played right into Amber hands. His land was ripe for the taking. In a major industry of the country, the small vigneron had a poor chance of survival. It was regrettable but certainly inevitable.

Of course as "family" he was given a place on the board and an excellent salary, but this was the artistic temperament. He was no tycoon. The Ambers were the tycoons: Luke, and his two sons, Richard and Guy. Richard, the elder, was killed when his horse fell and rolled on him on his father-in-law's property. The news, so sudden and tragic, heralded his father's massive stroke, though Luke Amber hovered on for several months between life and death before finally relinquishing his slender hold on life. After that, Guy Amber reigned supreme, second to no one, a position calling for courage, initiative and strong will. He possessed more than enough of all three. From all accounts, a man without a chink in his armour; a brilliant and successful business man, high-charged and ruthless, a ravening wolf that ate up timid little sheep.

But tragedy was not done with the Ambers. It ran its full cycle, striking in threes. Within a year Stephen Hartmann was killed, his death giving spate to a series of newspaper articles on the wealth and misfortunes of the Amber clan. The facts were printed, a few theories advanced. There had been a party at Belle Amber, which Stephen and Eva Hartmann had attended as a matter of course. They left early for a reason no two guests seemed able to agree upon. Yes, there had been some slight dissention, but certainly no blazing row. But no one, not even her mother, had known what was in Stephen Hartmann's mind when he piled up his silver grey sports car less than four miles from the house. The evening that had started out so brilliantly had ended literally and horribly – in a crash. Stephen had been killed instantly, his wife thrown clear, suffering multiple minor injuries.

Arguments were forgotten, and young as she was Karen had been aware of them. The family crowded around the bereaved widow, her two bewildered young children: Guy Amber and his sister, Patricia, almost desperately unhappy; Aunt Patricia, the children called her, though she was really their mother's cousin. Mark Amber, Luke Amber's only brother; Aunt Celia, Richard's widow, with her two children, Rikki and Liane. The uncles and the aunts and the cousins, all Amber shareholders and wonderfully eager to lend their wealth and support. Their mother had rejected them. With the ruthlessness and abandon of grief Eva Hartmann had cut herself off from her family, living out her life a bitter recluse. Karen's memories of her mother were based more on wishful thinking than reality, but her memories of her father were sweet. She stared down at his lean, handsome face, her dear father who had gone out of her life so quickly, so tragically. Something about his eyes gave her the feeling she was looking into a mirror. They were so much like her own, the same golden colour, slightly tilted under winging brows. His thick black hair was hers, the set of his head, the same cool elegance of bone structure.

It was then Karen knew a moment of sheer desperation. Her father had been such a champion of the young Guy Amber. He had liked and admired him, constantly applauded his extraordinary business acumen, far more pronounced than that of his tragic elder brother. Could Stephen Hartmann have been such a poor judge of character? Could she and Philip be the victims of their mother's warped judgment? Instantly Karen refuted the thought, and loyalty to her mother swung back like the tide. No, it couldn't be so! The letters proved it. Guy Amber was the black-hearted villain she had always thought him. His image flashed before her eyes and her anger subsided like a pricked bubble. No, not always. Once in her childhood, he had been a sort of demi-god to her, with an aura of brilliance and sophistication. In those days he had fascinated her, though she had been careful to steer clear of him, for he was a merciless tease, fond of pulling her hair and calling her "cat's eyes".

She was torn between weeping and the desire to hate him. Memories one after the other thrust their way up from her subconscious and the past sprang to life again.

She was back at Belle Amber; the colour and shape of her existence, the most beautiful place on earth to her. Where the great vineyards stopped there was the house, white and enormous under its great curving roof, glowing with pride in its beauty and bounty. She had no resistance against the onslaught of its remembered fascination, and warmth flooded through her like a hot sun through the vineyards.

Once, every weekend, every school vacation had been spent at Belle Amber. All the children loved it – Karen and Rikki, Liane and Pip, the baby. How well she remembered the excitement at vintage time when visitors like pilgrims descended on the famous old show-place, eager to be initiated into the delights of the vintage; the ritual and the magic that attended the occasion – the right approach to good wine, her father had called it. In her mind's eye she could still see him, lazing back nonchalantly, his lean body relaxed watching the visitors holding their wine glasses, peering and frowning, gyrating the wine around, some of them spilling it, the experts taking great thirsty gulps of it, the novices sipping, some smiling knowingly at some dazzling revelation, others full of fanciful descriptions that made his long mouth twist in a smile. Often he turned to Aunt Patricia with a quick witty comment, waiting for her answering smile; a smile that brought into play the most fascinating dimple at the side of her mouth.

Her mother never cared for showing visitors around and always avoided it by staying up at the house. Aunt Patricia loved it. So did her father and so did the children, ever eager to show off their knowledge, formidable enough for mere children. Even Guy Amber thought nothing of carrying a few flagons of Amber red out to a waiting car, his manner was charming and natural as any visitor could wish for.

Karen stood, faintly smiling, her thoughts turned inwards. In her fancy she could smell the odours of sweetness that emerged from the cellars; of fruit and soft oils and delicate ethers; acid smells and bitter smells, the sickly smell of fermenting juice, the vigorous bubbling and gurgling in the wax-lined concrete tanks, thickly capped with skins, pips and stalks – The Amber dry reds, the straight Cabernet Sauvigon, a wonderfully delicate table wine, made only in small quantities when conditions were favourable, and the more "forward" Shiraz-Cabernet, a "big" red, full bodied and fruity, but still retaining the distinctive Cabernet "nose" . . .

14

Philip had to call three times before Karen heard him. The thread of remembrance was snapped. She ran to the door, calling with sisterly conscientiousness – "Coming, pet, it'll only take a few minutes to heat up the casserole."

Two evenings later when Philip was long settled and Karen was busy correcting theory papers, the phone jangled. Karen put a paperweight over her work and went to answer it.

"Hello, Karen?" A woman's voice, clear and well modulated, came over the wires, a voice not entirely strange to her.

Karen answered politely. "Yes, Karen Hartmann speaking. Who is that?"

The mysterious, unidentifiable voice gave a slight husky laugh, one might have thought emotion-laden.

"Patricia Amber, my dear. Surely you remember me, Karen?"

"You have the wrong number, I'm sorry," Karen said with shocked disbelief, and hung up. The telephone rang again immediately, but she felt too depressed to answer it. Gently she took the receiver off the hook. It was no friend after all, she thought with a pang of regret. Meanwhile she was wasting time. She moved back into the living room. She had at least ten more papers to correct. As a teacher, at least, she thought rather sadly, she was successful. The overall standard was high.

She sat down again, to be startled twenty minutes later by the door chimes, shivering through the silence. Her head jerked up. There was no need for alarm; there was a chain on the door. She went to answer it, not even pausing to smooth back her dark, tumbled hair.

A man stood on the threshold; thirty-five or thereabouts – a tall, powerfully built man, but lean. A man there was no question of passing unnoticed, for he had a kind of dark splendour on him; the nose straight and classic, the cheek and jawline angular, too strong for easy good looks. Power and self-assurance seemed to flow from him and showed itself in the set of his head, and his shoulders, even more in the alive intelligence of his face, the alert and brilliant dark eyes. Karen almost recoiled in astonishment, her breath coming jaggedly. All her life, whatever else she forgot she would always remember this man. His eyes glittered over her. She felt the jolt of their impact right through her body.

"What the devil do you mean by hanging up on Patricia? You upset her dreadfully." His deep, arrogant voice almost struck at her physically, as compelling as a hidden current. "Open the door, Karen. I must speak to you." His tone was urgent, but there was nothing welcoming about his appearance, she thought bleakly. Those black brows and high cheekbones portrayed an alien, rather inhuman quality.

Her heart gave a great lunge and antagonism raced in her blood.

"How dare you come here!" she burst out passionately, her emotions ravaged to the point where she thought she couldn't stand it. "This is my home and no Amber will ever set foot in it. There's no magic formula to wash away the years ... the tears that have been shed for you. Please go away. There's nothing to say. How could you think otherwise?"

His tone was impersonal. There was an ironic aloofness to the twist of his mouth.

"I see the blood line hasn't weakened over the years. Eva speaks through her daughter. Open this door, child. I'm not prepared to lay myself out on your doorstep." His eyes flickered over her stricken young face and his voice underwent a distinct change, became subtly insistent, easing the tone of authority. She almost gave him an "A" for adjustment.

"Please hear me out, Karen. I only want to help you, though you've been well taught to loathe and resent me."

Karen shivered on a great wave of helplessness. The quiet, level tone had more authority than a shout. He was so very smooth, so convincing, she knew it would be futile, even undignified to put up a further show of resistance. He was a man quick to rouse and she knew without question that his tem-

16

per would be something to watch. It was too much! too much! too much!

She shot back the lock and he was through the door as swiftly as any hunter, towering above her. She was trapped, with the momentary impression of a magnificent black panther absolved from the ordinary rules and customs. The light shone down on his raven head. His dark eyes pinned her gaze.

"You haven't changed. You're like Stephen ... to look at! You have his eyes, his bone structure, his good looks distilled. One day you'll be beautiful." His brilliant dark gaze shifted. "Let's go in, Karen. I've things to discuss with you." He held out his hand and with the force of her outraged emotions Karen retreated from him, avoiding contact. The woman was born in her, fully formed and ready to fight him, even if it proved fatal.

He was unused to opposition of any kind. His steely grip encircled her wrist as he stopped her retreat. She had the frightening sensation that anything Guy Amber wanted he would never let go of. His voice almost crackled with impatience as he gazed down at her tumbled dark head.

"Don't be afraid, Karen. I'd never hurt you!"

"I'm *not* afraid!" she muttered fiercely, looking him over deliberately with the same piercing appraisal he had bestowed on her.

He looked down into her over-bright eyes, observing every small detail of her upturned face.

"No, damn it, I don't believe fear comes easily to you. So much the better for both of us. In here, then, you colourful child." He drew her into the living room as though she and the house were already his chattels, then gave her a slight push into an armchair and sat down opposite her, his eyes not ungentle, but piercingly intent.

"Now, let's try to clear up all these distortions and confusions that are troubling you. Why did you never answer my letters? Surely common courtesy hasn't gone out of style?"

She gave a short, jerky laugh, gripping the arms of her chair.

"Oh, really, this is insufferable! You force your way in here ... into my home. Surely you weren't planning on an effusive chat? It's been so long and all that ... Well, let me tell you you've materialised a little too suddenly for my comfort. There's no kindness or sentiment in you, only a devilish cunning. You're hard and unyielding, a real Machiavelli, with an ominous face and black brows drawn, and I just know you could be violent and wild given the chance." Tension and excitement curved about her like a bright banner.

His voice cut across hers with the incredibly quiet command.

"Stop all that fanciful nonsense and get a hold on yourself, child. You're becoming over-emotional." There was a hint of real concern in his searching dark eyes. "For once in your young life, listen to fact and not preconceived notions. This is painful, I know, but it can't be glossed over. The old days are past. Your mother has gone. Eva was the victim of her own difficult nature. She was a bitter, unhappy woman who punished herself and punished us all in the process. She would never allow us to see you, you and Philip. You must remember how much the family loved both of you. She cut you out of our lives, yet she had no qualms about taking the money I sent her."

His words were a bright lick of flame towards dynamite. They exploded in her ears, sharp and vivid as lightning. She sprang at him then, the hectic colour staining her cheekbones. He came to his feet precipitately at the sight of her slight flying body, catching her under both elbows, and she felt the steely strength of his fingers through her thin sweater, a curious throbbing where his hands touched her.

"You're lying!" she blazed up at him, her face vivid with outraged pride. "I simply don't believe you. Mother would never take money from you. Not money ... not anything. I know. We've had to struggle for years, I tell you."

His dark face was formidable, a muscle moved tautly along

18

his jawline. "I never lie, little one. There was no struggle, believe me."

Her heart thumped erratically, as though it could not contain itself within the confines of her body. He was too tall, too powerful, too able to reduce to nonsense her most deeply rooted opinions.

"You're the enemy, I know," she said coldly, "but you'll never daunt me. I'll be no pawn in your power game. My mother *was* a bitter, unhappy woman, I know that. She was weighed down with grief and regrets. She lived out her life withdrawn from society, but she carried her own burden, isolated from her family – a family she could no longer trust. I have the same pride, the same sense of dignity, and I absolutely demand my own privacy."

He studied her for a long moment, faintly intrigued as though she was something quite unique in his experience. When he spoke his voice was almost indulgent.

"I can see you believe in taking the devil by his horns as though there were no other way."

"There *is* no other way," she burst out impetuously. "Surely you can see that? You're a business man. Cut your losses. You'll gain nothing from me, though you'll do anything to achieve your purpose. Lie about it if you have to, as you've done in the past !"

A strange expression flared in his brilliant dark eyes.

"What an insolent child you are, Karen. The prospect of taking you in hand begins to appeal to me."

She wore a soft, ironic smile. "I make no apology for saying what I think."

"You'll find I'm without apology either." His hands tightened on her experimentally. "Just remember, my little firebrand, hot tempers are a characteristic of the Ambers, so our skirmishes won't be always this one-sided."

Her response was commendably cool for a young girl. She moved back and away from him, curling up in an armchair, her expression brightening with triumph.

"Perhaps not. But I'll always fall outside your circle of influence. Being a male and an Amber you won't recognise it, I know, but it's a fact all the same, an unshakable fact of nature."

She looked very young and very graceful against the gold velvet of the old wing-backed chair. A smile, white and transforming, crossed his sombre dark face.

"And what would you know about 'unshakable facts of nature' my little innocent – and you *are* an innocent, for all the exotic tilt to your eyebrows. The closest you've ever come to nature is a school project, by the look of you. You've never in your life seen a man as an individual, only as a symbol. Right now, I'm the symbol of tyranny in your young life, the hateful Guy Amber, the villain in a melodrama. Well, let's make a bargain, my stubborn young relative. I'll allow you to go your way entirely at Belle Amber, of course, if you'll allow me to do my best for Philip. As I remember, he's *all* Amber."

"He has the family cast of features, if that's what you mean," she said cuttingly. "But thank God, that's as far as it goes."

"Karen, Karen!" He gave a mocking sigh, his hand slowly clenching. "Young as you are, you almost demolish me. Quite an accomplishment! Now listen, you temperamental young woman. However well you've been brainwashed, it can't all be true. Surely you've collected a few facts along the line? It just can't all be true. My sister Patricia is a wonderful woman. You must remember her. You were very fond of her when you were a child. Even if you would never come near me. I remember very well a ponytailed little brat with great golden irises, the exact colour of cognac." He was smiling at her in the old remembered way, his beautiful dark eyebrows arching.

She looked at him strangely, swinging to hide a sharp deep breath.

"Don't turn away from me, now, Karen," he said softly.

The colour drained from her ivory skin. He was too strong

20

for her, his brand of charm too compelling. His speaking voice was very beautiful and her musical ear was fast succumbing to its dark velvet tones. No doubt he found it an invaluable aid in his big business ventures.

He studied her profile, then leant over and picked up her wrist, turning her hand over to examine her slender, oval-tipped fingers.

"Your hands have a strange vitality to them," he murmured, "almost as though they had a life of their own. You use them so much when you speak. Stephen used to do that." Abruptly his voice recaptured its usual pitch. "Don't waste your life for a shadow, Karen. I want to look after you, you and young Philip. I've always wanted to, though I don't expect you to believe me right now. You've been conditioned to hate me in your formative years."

A deep flush swept up from her throat. He was too near the mark. His lean, long-fingered hands against her skin were sending warning signals to her brain. The queerest sensation like excitement threatened to catch her up in a vice. It was making itself felt throughout her whole body. She knew with finality that he was the most sensual man she would ever be likely to meet.

Her pride made her cry out in resistance. "But I do hate you, there's no question about that, and you're only seeing the tip of the iceberg. There are fiercer, deeper resentments I'm hiding."

His face changed subtly.

"You're not meant to hate, little one. Not with your eyes and mouth." He released her hand lightly. "You know in your heart that you and Philip need my protection. You're only a young girl, alone, trying to rear a small boy. Even if I take care of all your expenses it's still not enough." His eyes swung about the mellowed beauty of the room. The light fell along his dark profile, remote and strongly aquiline. He had the look of a man deep in reverie, the dark head arrogant, the mouth sensuously beautiful, somehow conveying an impression of faint sardonic amusement. Yet there was a suggestion of something completely devoid of amusement about him as though the face could contain, at one and the same time, two powerful conflicting forces. It was, Karen concluded almost fearfully, an unforgettable face.

His voice jarred her out of her dream world.

"You must play for me," he said quietly, almost under his breath, his eyes on the gleaming Steinway.

"You assume rather a lot, don't you?" she made her voice sound light and amused. "I never said I *could* play. That was my father's piano, remember?"

His dark eyes came back to her, narrowing.

"*You* play," he said with quiet emphasis. He took in her young classically oval face, ivory and intense with the promise of great beauty. His eyes fastened on her full, deeply moulded mouth, trembling with barely concealed emotion. "Strange how sadness points up beauty," he said almost musingly. "There's a great deal of hurt and a great deal of tenderness in those great golden eyes. But you're only awaiting a touch spark of some challenge to burst into flame. Do you realise it, I wonder?" He used a tone that implied a certain tenderness and Karen moved restlessly, frightened and wary of his easy mastery.

She had no wish to respond to such provocation, so she withdrew from it. She swung her eyes away from him, deliberately fixing her attention on a curtain that swayed erratically on the night breeze. He seemed to be making a conscious effort to taunt and tantalise her. She hadn't the experience to cope with it.

He looked at her for a long moment, her dark eyes unfathomable, noting the expression on her young face at once moody and sad. Abruptly his voice picked up.

"Now how long will it take you to finalise things here, Karen? Your job, etc. I'll arrange the sale of the house. It's in need of attention, but it's a beautiful old place and the site is excellent. I'll have no bother at all disposing of it and it should bring you in a nice little independence. Send the piano on when you're ready, and I'll settle the account at the other end. Have it tuned before you arrive."

All at once Karen felt the tears threatening. It was the final humiliation. All her old feeling for him, for Belle Amber crystallised into an intense longing and need. But it had to be denied. The words bubbled painfully, desperately, to the surface.

"I can't possibly agree. It's all wrong, I tell you. Mother would turn in her grave. If you knew ... Mother ... the Ambers ... I can't bear all your convincing diplomacy. It's too studied, too dangerous." She broke off half chokingly and found herself in his arms. Her head found the curve of his shoulder and her body quivered pathetically against his lean, powerful frame. Suddenly she knew the most overwhelming compulsion to draw strength from this hard, vital man. All the world spun around in a circle with the two of them its pulsating centre. The silence was so complete it rang in her ears. Gradually, awareness closed in on her, the almost relentless magnetism that was emanating from him. She pulled away frantically, biting hard on her underlip. She tasted blood in her mouth and came to her senses.

"I'm sorry," she said curtly, sounding just the opposite.

His mouth compressed slightly.

"There's no need to apologise, though that's the first time I've ever been able to endure a weeping woman. But you're not a woman yet, are you? Just a girl-into-woman – a dangerous combination." He swivelled her to face him again. "Don't fight me, little one. Not now, not ever. I'll always look after you if only you'll let me. Think of Philip even if you deny your own right to security and happiness. Philip, I remember, used to love Belle Amber though he was only a baby. It's part of his heritage, after all."

"But surely you're married . . . have children. You used to be so . . ."

"Sought after?" he supplied, his hard mouth ironic. "I still have my moments, little one, but I can't say I've ever met the woman to hold my attention . . . for as long as it's necessary, anyway." His dark eyes were worldly and glittering. "We may never be exactly *simpatico*, but at least give me your promise of loyalty."

"I give it where it's due," she said cuttingly. A fierce sort of tautness held her immobile. She was fully prepared for this moment. It had been a long time coming.

Harsh sardonic humour leapt in his eyes.

"How you do play havoc with my ego, child! I can see I'll have to move warily."

"At least it's nice to know you *do* have a weakness," she countered smoothly. "You seem so incredibly steely. I take heart from it."

His hand closed over the tender slope of her shoulder.

"I was thinking of finding you some nice young man to cope with your humours, but I can see that would never do. I'm not at all sure a nice young man would survive that débâcle. You definitely need a master."

Some instinct made her shake herself free of him, angered and confused by her response to physical contact.

"I think not," she said hardily. "That kind of man would only meet with unrelenting resistance."

His eyes, long-fringed, gleamed with cool speculation.

"Do you think so? You look extraordinarily young and tormented at the moment, as though opposing forces were conspiring to tear you apart. You're going to take life hard, little one. That's why I want to be around."

She looked up at him, her black brows arching, her white skin curiously incandescent under the light.

"To give a devil his due, you do know how to manage your affairs. You almost have me persuaded. But then your voice is

24

a powerful weapon, as I'm sure you've been told by that train of inadequate ladies who failed to hold your attention. Philip as a potential heir is a nice touch, too."

His eyes deepened to jet and a sudden menace glittered in them.

"Don't tempt hell fire, little one. I'll take just so much from you."

She didn't move her great golden eyes from his face. "Why the sudden flare-up?" she mocked him silkily. "Surely you've been insulted before?"

"By experts," he drawled, his eyes on the tell-tale pulse, that beat in her throat, "among whom I wouldn't concede you a chance."

"I've managed up until now," she managed with an air of youthful bravado, the colour flaring in her cheeks.

"That might change at any moment." His hard mouth relaxed. "Don't trade too hard on your sex, little one. Try to handle its privileges discreetly."

"To please whom?" she retorted swiftly.

"Me!" His dark eyes were amused. "It would be a step in the right direction." His eyes flickered over her tempestuous young face. "With the right clothes, the right make-up, that dark mane of yours under control, you'll be quite an acquisition to the family, a rather exotic sophisticate."

Surprise jerked her to a standstill.

"Have you ever contemplated a course of action that excluded personal gain?"

He flicked a hand to her cheekbones, his eyes deep as rapids.

"You defeat me entirely, child. It's a new experience. But let's sink our differences, if only for Philip's sake. He needs a man's hand, a man's discipline, not so much now but in a year or two. Make your break and return to Belle Amber. I promise not to stamp out all that marvellous fire."

Her lashes were heavy crescents on her cheek.

"I'm sorry. You make it sound very enticing, but I can't

25

answer. I need time. I can't adjust so rapidly." Already with a sick heart Karen knew she was weakening. To pledge her loyalty to the Ambers would be to turn her back on the past. Yet how could she subdue this overwhelming sense of guilt, though her mother was no longer there to be distressed and affected by it? She felt suddenly as if she were a child with a child's ideas of right and wrong, rigidly separated. But nothing was so clear cut as that: there were always the fine shadings, the blurred edges. Grand gestures had a habit of turning self-defeating. Her mother had virtually destroyed herself with her implacable attitude.

He was quick to see the confusion of thought in her face.

"Don't think too deeply about things, Karen. It's an exhausting sport at the best of times. Right now you're suffering from a first reaction. Tomorrow you'll be over the crisis, adjusted to the idea. Then one day when you're in a more receptive mood I'll try to explain what really broke up our two families. Family quarrels are the worst quarrels of all, but you're not ready to hear about it yet." His voice ran on, disarming as a lullaby. "You can be as independent as you like. It's your nature, I can see that, but not for twenty-four hours a day, my child. It's too much, and you're only a girl. I want to look after you. Perhaps we're two of a mould. If we are it's in the logic of things that we should pull together. It would make a certain kind of sense from all the chaos. Come back to Belle Amber, Karen. It's even more beautiful than you remember."

She raised her faintly tip-tilted eyes to him with almost drugged acceptance, conscious of the frightening pleasure his presence gave her. But his attractions were not to be trusted.

"I'll come," she said quickly, not giving herself a chance to turn back. "But only for Philip. He deserves a great deal more than I can give him, though I'd try very hard. He's my reason for living, the most important person in the world to me."

His gaze swept over her, strangely insistent.

"You're so young," he said almost wearily, his dark face

26

taciturn. He moved swiftly, then drawing her with him to the front door. He paused with his hand on the polished knob looking down at her. "Don't keep me waiting, Karen. It's already been far too long!"

For an instant she looked up at him, caught into a moment of deep familiarity. His face had haunted her for so long and now he was here in front of her. He took her hand, his fingers tightening a little.

"You have to win in the end, don't you?" she said softly, the irony creeping back into her tone. "It's not very fair!"

"Life is never very fair, Karen," he said, looking directly into her eyes. "But couldn't you be honest for once, little one, and admit you're winning too?"

A sudden warmth sparked in her cheeks and her heart flipped half crazily. How frightening he was! Yet weren't all exciting people rather frightening? She was sure her jumble of emotions must show in her face.

"I think we'll be able to tolerate one another," he said lazily, his mouth curving.

"In small doses," she amended, and slanted a smile at him, her hand making a charming and provocative little gesture. Some force in her went rushing out to meet him compulsively, elementally, trapped in the quicksand of his strange fascination. Always imaginative, she couldn't suppress the strangest conviction that she was being guided in an inexplicable manner towards her destiny, some very queer intention of fate that brought Guy Amber back into her life again. The moment spun out, snatched out of time and fraught with significance.

His eyes shifted to the lovely curve of her mouth.

"No, a nice young man won't do at all, Karen," he said briefly, then opened the door and walked down into the night, one hand raised in a parting salute.

Karen stood for a long moment looking after him. She felt a stranger, even to herself, with a calm she could not understand, almost complete in itself. The garden was a blue-black jungle after the blazing shimmer of the house, and the air had a special sweet freshness of a cool night with an expected overnight shower. Against the white fence the yellow forsythia's sprays were silvered by moonlight. The magnolia tree in the corner was no more than a dark shadow waiting for springtime. In another month it would be heavy with flowers and fragrance. Even the grass was springing to new life. A solitary willy wagtail let fall five crystal-clear notes like a cascade of broken glass. It was the final touch of magic. The whole world was awakening from a long sleep!

CHAPTER II

Spring had come to Belle Amber. The sun shone gold and benign on the ripening young grapes, line upon line, plunging on the vines, their shiny leaves, healthy and luxuriant, rippling like a vast green sea. Two hundred acres flourished in the foothills, set to the heavy bearing Shiraz and the "shyer" Cabernet Sauvignon, the aristocratic grape of Bordeaux.

The timing of the first green pruning had been perfect, a combination of experience and instinct, and the weather at the spring flowering free from high wind with just sufficient rain to fill out the berries without swelling them – with water, not flavour. All that remained was a spell of hot weather to ripen the grapes and develop the sugars – the potential alcohol. With any luck at all it would be a vintage year.

The great wrought iron gates leading to the house stood open and Guy Amber stopped the car at the entrance. Karen caught her breath, profoundly stirred. The high arch of lacy grillework hung on tall formal pillars and framed a long sweeping driveway, flanked by poplars; poplars that wore the traditional delicate green of spring. Up ahead was the house. Karen was filled with the urgent desire to see it. The man at her side turned to study her profile, her dream-shadowed eyes. He slid his arm along the back of the seat, amused and indulgent at the effect the first sight of the estate was having upon her.

"I can see from your face that Belle Amber is working the same old magic."

Philip's clear young voice piped up on the silence.

"I'll say it is, it's beaut, Uncle Guy! I swear I remember it." He leaned over from the back seat and thrust his dark head between them. "Do you mind if I walk up to the house, Uncle

29

Guy? I've got a cramp in my foot – wouldn't you know it! A bit of a run might fix it."

Guy Amber laughed and swung his arm back to open the door.

"Go right ahead. This is your home now, Pip. I want you to enjoy it. Get to know every inch of it."

"Gee, thanks, Uncle Guy." Philip's young face reflected his liking and admiration for this re-found relative. He dashed out on to the pebbled drive and began banging his foot strenuously a half a dozen times. When his circulation was restored to his satisfaction he gave his sister a quick grin, then ran up ahead, disappearing into the bend of the drive with a backward wave of his hand.

Karen was silent, feeling curiously deserted. An awareness of the man at her side closed in on her thick as a cloud. He smiled at her averted profile.

"I was determined you would see it now when it's so beautiful with the spring flowering. The estate is beautiful at any time, but never quite like this."

She gave him a quick glance, fighting off an inexplicable surge of emotion at this obvious sign of his desire to please her. Illogically she resented it. She let her glance rest on him with cool intent, reflecting that there were three qualities that exactly personified this man: an almost regal assurance, determination and an aura of intense masculinity.

She gave him a swift unpremeditated answer: "Beware the gift that's laid in your hands – the frightening gift of happiness." Her eyes flicked his dark face. "Under that facile charm I sense a certain ruthlessness. Your *words* charm me, but I know I ought to mistrust the man behind them."

He gave a derisive little laugh. "How wonderfully direct you are, Karen!" The quality of his laugh, amused and forbearing, fired her temper, and indignation made the words come tumbling out.

"Diametrically opposed to you, perhaps. I wonder what

category you'd fall into. I'd say you were clever and devious and . . ." she broke off in alarm, stirred and excited, as one lean hand encircled her throat.

"You were saying?" he inquired pleasantly. "Clever and devious and . . ." The broad shoulders moved slightly nearer her.

"There are some situations in life one must just accept," she murmured obliquely, a lingering after glow in her cheeks from his touch.

"And this is one of them." He let the seconds tick by, then tapped her cheek lightly.

"It is funny how things work out though, isn't it?" she persisted, not very humorously.

A smile tugged at his mouth. "Funny is hardly the word, Karen. It's utterly amazing."

"And I simply have to rise above it, though it might just prove too much for *you*." Her voice danced over the tension that flared between them.

His dark eyes were coolly confident.

"I never undertake a venture I'm not capable of handling, little one. It might help you to remember it."

Her red, passionate mouth was ironic. "I could hardly fail to, could I? Your voice is loaded with conviction." She sighed elaborately. "It must be wonderful to be so self-assured. Then I imagine you sprang from the cradle fully armoured."

The laugh he sent across to her was sardonic.

"If you're not careful, my little cat, you'll finish with a tongue like carbolic acid."

She had the grace to blush. "Making me therefore a completely undesirable female."

His glance licked over her like a flame. "Did I say that? No, Karen. With a little wisdom, a little maturity you'll draw men like candlelight draws moths."

She moved her shining dark head in denial. "You make that sound an unworthy accomplishment. In any case, you're speaking to a girl only too anxious to avoid trouble."

"And men are trouble?"

"Some men," she murmured under her breath. "There are others, good and kind and generous."

"Good gracious, that sounds like an obituary!" he taunted her lazily.

"You mustn't heed my sense of humour," she said crisply.

His dark eyes gleamed. "For a girl who's anxious to avoid trouble, you seem to court danger as a matter of course. I'd better take the car up the drive, if only to avert another of your haymakers."

She glanced over swiftly at his arrogant dark profile, letting her gaze travel over the casual perfection of his jacket, the elegant cut and beautiful fabric.

He turned his own head, pinning her gaze, and some dark force, some probing light in his eyes held her still. Ashamed and grieved, she recognised her sensuous delight in the sight and the scent of him, the very sound of his beautifully timbred voice. But it was the traitor touch! She dared not raise the curtain on her own blossoming instincts or their implications. Guy Amber was simply a man, handsome and successful, with a sexual radiance that most women would instantly recognise. Once she accepted this self-evident fact she would be able to put it safely out of her head. She took a deep, even breath, pretending a casualness she did not feel. "Anything you say, oh, stern-faced lord of the manor!"

He smiled and leaned forward to switch on the ignition. The engine purred into life and his lean, strong fingers closed around the wheel. The car started and the pebbles crunched and sprayed out from under the tyres. They swept up the tree-shaded drive and Karen sat forward a lovely, eager light in her eyes. This was where she belonged! Aware of her rising excitement, Guy changed gear to let the car cruise gently through vast spreads of sloping lawn that led to a crest. On the crest stood Belle Amber; the dream had materialised and the magic she had counted lost returned.

It rose, up ahead, snow-white and perfect; a colonial mansion built in the early days of settlement by Matthew Amber, a wealthy Englishman, for his French bride, Julienne. When the colony of South Australia was first advertised, Matthew Amber sold up his Californian vineyards and migrated, along with his entire household, to this vast new-found continent. Within a month he had purchased fifty acres in the Adelaide foothills and set the land to the vine. As the years went by he acquired more land, more prestige; planted more vines; made still better wines and devoted himself through a long lifetime to the art of the vigneron. Such was the beginning of the great trading company of Amber Estates Ltd.

Softly Karen held her voice steady under her pounding blood.

"Already I love it. . . ."

"More than yesterday and less than tomorrow." He flicked a glance over her creamy face, at once dreamy and burningly alive. The very curve of her neck spelled enchantment. His voice was almost tender. "Welcome back to Belle Amber, Karen. You look quite different, do you know that? Young and terribly eager, completely untouched by conflict, the way you were meant to look. The way I like you to look."

She could feel her heart beating rapidly. Stop it, she thought. Look away from those dark eyes, the splendid dark head. Unsell your own senses if you have to. It can be done. It has to be done. He's just a fascinating man, older and unattainable. Besides, he wasn't to be trusted. She looked away with a sense of purpose, deliberately veiling her eyes with a faraway look.

"A penny for your thoughts?" he said lightly, then smiled at her flicker of discomfort. "Ten cents, then."

"They're not worth the first offer, I'm afraid."

His dark eyes met hers across the space that divided them.

"Do something for me, Karen. Meet Patricia again without any preconceived notions. Just greet her naturally. She's longing to have you and young Philip. Be kind to her."

33

She looked over at him, her great eyes reproachful.

"What a strange thing to say to me! Surely you don't imagine I'll play the proud lady. Marie Antoinette condescending
to the mob."

He laughed gently. "What a graphic child you are! No,
Karen, I didn't mean quite that. But you could be a cruel little
cat with someone's heart in your hands."

She withdrew from him visibly. "You do me an injustice.
I have no taste for such things, unlike the ladies of your acquaintance."

"Perhaps not, Karen, but we're only at the beginning of re-
discovery. Patricia is different ... strangely vulnerable. You
and Philip will be special to her. If it's any comfort at all to you,
you're really needed at Belle Amber."

Her eyes registered every detail of his dominant dark face.

"How clever you are! You've hit on the lure by which we
are all irresistably trapped ... to be needed. Just the one phrase
– you're needed, Karen."

"And so you are, little one. All you have to do is let time
clear up your past impressions. It takes living with people, seeing them involved in the process of day-to-day living, to give
them their true dimension."

She looked at him steadily, her topaz eyes gleaming. "We all
have a sprinkle of saint and sinner."

He intercepted her line of thought exactly. "Now *you* have
the makings of a rather spectacular temper. You should make
a formidable old lady."

Karen shook her dark head in denial. "You invest too much
meaning in my casual word."

He laughed softly. "Karen, Karen, even you don't believe
that. Already you see yourself as a flaming sword between me
and all worthy causes."

Suddenly, with a shrug, she yielded.

"Forgive me, Guy," she said slowly, speaking more sweetly
than she intended.

His smile was sardonic. "That *Guy* was more potent than wine. I can see you don't play for playing – but for winning."

She shrugged rather helplessly. "We seem to have been having this kind of conversation since we met."

His eyes smiled at her. "You mean we've cut through all the polite preliminaries. One day you'll be quite a woman, Karen!"

"Praise indeed. But in my own mind at least, I'm already a woman." Her tone, young and ardent, settled all arguments.

His handsome face was disbelieving. "Never, child. A woman's not really a woman until she's had a man's arms round her." Instinct made her move back against the seat, her head bent, her cheeks colouring.

"You're far too worldly for me."

"Beyond all question." He smiled at her with elaborate taunting courtesy, making her look away excited and confused. Guy Amber was dangerous with an almost relentless magnetism. The conviction had come and come for keeps.

"Relax, little one," he ordered briefly, "you're as taut as a bowstring."

Obediently Karen rested her head against the plush, expensive-smelling upholstery, releasing her pent-up breath.

As they drew abreast of the house Guy veered to the right where an enormous four-car garage presented three closed doors and a yawning black maw. As they eased into the garage she had the clear impression of orderly kept tools and gardening equipment and a long low sports car wedged between two much bigger cars. Guy opened the door and came round for her, taking her elbow. They walked from the garage around towards the front of the house and mounted the wide shallow steps to the colonnaded porch that ran the entire length of the two-storied central wing.

Through the open entrance hall Karen glimpsed the patina of lustrous veneer, the gleaming parquet floor and the beautiful curving stairway that sprang up from the centre of the hall and wound its way into the upper storey. From the high-flung plastered ceiling hung a great chandelier dripping crystals that made ghostly music in the breeze.

Karen was aware of her own mounting tension and tried to relax it. Unconsciously she moved closer to Guy Amber, who encircled her wrist imposing on her the lightest restraint.

"You're poised to spring like a doe in the forest, Karen. Relax. I promise you this will be easy."

She suppressed her half-formed wish to flee.

"Now I'm here I dread it as much as I desire it."

"Hush now!" he held her still.

Even as he spoke a woman emerged from the interior of the house, hurrying towards them with swinging grace. She came on swiftly, smiling as she came.

"Karen!" Her voice made Karen's name a sound of purest delight. Trembling slightly with a jumble of emotions, Karen stared at her, seeing a tall, over-slender woman in her early forties with the ageless kind of beauty on her, and whose strong physical resemblance to Guy Amber instantly proclaimed her his sister – Patricia Amber.

Instantly Karen's mind was stormed with scenes from her childhood; scenes in which this woman had played so large a part. The dark, luminous eyes were fixed on her face, seemingly trying to look into her very heart. Patricia Amber, the faintly sinister, illusory figure of the past eight years, existed no longer. She had not the remotest connections with this dark-haired, graceful woman who wore charm and humour and great personal dignity like a cloak.

She stood holding out her hand and for a second Karen hesitated, then her instincts took over from her. She was impelled forward and found herself caught in a warm embrace, betrayed into a depth of response she found herself helpless to conceal. The dark eyes that looked back at her were blurred with emotion.

Patricia Amber stood back a little, surveying her young relative with sparkling, totally approving eyes. "Why, Karen darling, didn't I always say you would be beautiful, and you're so like . . ." she took a deep steadying breath, half laughing, half crying, "so like . . ."

"Stephen!" Guy Amber intervened gently, putting a hand on his sister's shoulder.

She brushed her cheek against it, drawing comfort from his touch, so it seemed to Karen. The dark eyes were glistening. "Pip has just rushed out after Uncle Mark. He wants one good look at the vineyard to be sure he's not dreaming. They'll be back shortly. I'm so grateful Guy was able to persuade you to come back to us, Karen."

Karen tilted her head, her eyes narrowing. "I don't suppose it occurred to Guy for one moment that he wouldn't succeed. He seems to be confident as few men are confident that he always gets his way."

"It's only a front, little one," Guy replied smoothly, though his eyes gleamed through their thick dark lashes. His sister caught hold of Karen's hand to draw her into the house.

"Come in, dear. I've so much to show you. We've had a whole suite redecorated for you, with Pip close by. I do want you to be happy here."

In the living room masses of fresh flowers were everywhere, conveying a deep sweet sense of homecoming. Dark polished wood contrasted with the ice blue sheen of damask-covered walls, while tall windows hung with a matching brocade, sent patterns of light over beautiful needlepoint rugs, velvet and silk upholstered pieces of mahogany and rosewood, and two beautiful Chippendale sofas. The whole effect was of elegance and a muted liveable beauty as though it had always been like that. And indeed it seemed to Karen as though nothing had changed. Paintings hung on the wall, expertly placed to enhance their colour and quality; landscapes, genre paintings, all very valuable, and an excellent portrait of old Matthew Amber. Karen felt a thrill of pride in that remarkable old face, with its strong angular cheekbones, the piercing dark eyes and silvery mane.

It was a remarkable face, full of character and a splendid life force. He looked what he was: a man of vision with the practical qualities to make the vision a reality.

Karen's eyes swept on round the room with increasing pleasure. Objects both striking and delicate were strewn around the room like so many jewels adorning low tables and chests, and lending warmth and personality – the intimate touch – to the great formal room.

Patricia Amber followed her eyes, smiling. "Everything beautiful is made of a mixture, so Plato tells us. As a family I think we've followed the idea through. We're all of us addicted to our 'pieces'. By the way, dear, Celia and Liane will be home Friday evening. Liane has just got herself engaged, but I'll let her tell you all about it. Rikki is here, of course. He's not as strong as we would like him to be after that bout of rheumatic fever when he was a child. He spends most of his time painting. Celia's equipped him with a first class studio, but we're not often favoured with the results. He's very secretive about it all." She turned to her brother, whose dark eyes were for once expressionless.

"Would you mind giving him a call, Guy?"

Karen intervened quickly, "Please don't bother on my account. There's no need to disturb him. Most artists hate an intrusion into their private world."

The short laugh Guy gave was unmistakably sardonic, but he turned away without comment. Patricia Amber watched him go, then turned back to Karen.

"I told Uncle Mark to be back by lunchtime. He's taken Pip on a tour of the vineyards." Her eyes brightened. "Oh, Karen, it is lovely to have you here!"

Karen's eyes never left her face. "You really mean that, don't you, Aunt Patricia?"

The dark eyes melted. "My dear child, having you and Pip is a great joy to me. Pip, I think, is like all our family, but you are your father. He lives on in you, Karen. You're extraordinarily like him. The same bones . . . the tilt of the eyes and the brows, even his trick of the hands. You bring him back so vividly." Her face was grave. "I was grieved by your mother's death, Karen. I want you to believe that. Eva had a most unhappy life, yet had circumstances been different she would have made an outstanding woman. She had it in her. We were very close as girls. I knew her so well." She sat for a moment seemingly lost in reflection. Karen looked at her downbent head, and wondered, not for the first time, at the exact part Patricia Amber had played in her mother's life. It was obvious that she was very devoted to her brother and he to her.

At that moment Guy Amber came back into the room, followed by a slender young man wearing paint-daubed jeans and a vivid blue shirt exposing a smooth golden expanse of chest. His hair was an authentic silver-gilt and tumbled artlessly-artful over his forehead and almost into his eyes, the exact colour of aquamarines. He looked a golden boy, intense and picturesque and to Karen's eyes astonishingly healthy. The vivid eyes found Karen's, slid over her with truly professional interest, before he broke into an appreciative whistle.

"Karo, Karo, I'm not sure if you haven't grown into the most beautiful bird in the world!" He covered the length of the room in the shortest possible time, grasping both of her hands. "Welcome back, little cat That's what Guy used to call you, remember. Or was it cat's eyes?"

"Something like that," Guy Amber drawled lazily.

Rikki was talking, the words tumbling out enthusiastically. "What a wonderful subject you'll make for me, Karo. The vivid contrast between your hair and eyes – it's quite stirring. Fancy picking a winner, and on my own home-ground. It's truly amazing!"

"You look wonderful to me, too, Rikki," Karen intervened gently, and on an impulse leant forward and kissed his cheek. It was smooth and golden and smelled faintly of turpentine. To her surprise he turned his head swiftly and kissed her mouth,

39

his own mouth warm and surprisingly sweet.

"Your affectionate nature does you credit, Rikki," Guy Amber drawled his words lazily. "Now I can safely leave Karen under your wing." He glanced over at his sister. "I won't be able to stay to lunch, Trish. I'm cutting it fine as it is. I may stay overnight in town and ring you in the morning." He gave Karen a charming half smile. "This time tomorrow, little one, you'll be fully absorbed into the household."

The gallantry of his words belied by the mocking light in his eyes. She met those eyes briefly.

"Thank you for meeting us. I do realise you have many demands on your time."

He tut-tutted gently. "That sounds excessively correct, Karen, and not at all like you." He reached for his car keys and jiggled them nonchalantly. "Walk out to the car with me, Trish. I've a few things to tell you. Rikki will look after Karen." The dark eyes veered towards his nephew. "Don't *overdo* it, Rikki."

Rikki coloured furiously. "You're the very devil, Guy!"

"So I've been told." He took hold of his sister's arm and guided her out into the hall, with a brief "goodbye."

Rikki returned to his silent scrutiny.

"Now we're alone, I want to tell you, I really mean what I say. You've grown very beautiful, Karo, and best of all you don't seem aware of it. Fantastic, that! Especially in this household. I've been racking my brains for weeks for the right subject for the Havilland Prize – you know, for portraiture. I'm determined to have a go at it and now you've arrived. A gift from the gods. Guy, of course, would have been marvellous. He's such a splendidly arrogant devil, but he'd never sit for me, not in a million years."

"Why not?" Karen found herself asking, hanging on the answer.

"You said it yourself, girl, he has too many demands on his time. He's really big business. I'm simply floored he went out of his way to pick you and Pip up. By the way, Pip's not unlike him, is he? The Amber features, I mean. I caught sight of him with Uncle Mark. He was dancing up and down firing questions. A bright sort of kid, thank God! Just the right sort for this household."

Karen decided to redirect his attention. "How good an artist are you, Rikki?"

He grinned deprecatingly. "Some days I think I'm damned good, well a cut above mediocre, other days I feel I've no show at all. But I'm ambitious, though I don't show the family much of my work. Not for a long time now. 'Rikki's little hobby', Celia calls it, and lets fall a crushing little tinkle of laughter."

"Celia? Your mother, you mean?" Karen's eyebrows shot up disbelievingly.

There was a wicked little grin on Rikki's face. "No one else, my sweet innocent. No one, least of all her own children, would dream of calling the exquisite Mrs. Celia Amber Mother. It's ageing, dear child, and too damn fundamental. Liane, poor thing, had to have it drummed into her. For me it came naturally. Still, I can't complain. She did set me up in the studio. It's safer to keep Rikki occupied, so he won't go gallivanting, pick up with girls, especially *pretty* girls. The Queen Bee doesn't tolerate competition. She can't take it, you know."

"That's absurd!" Karen protested faintly, feeling genuinely shocked.

Rikki's eyes narrowed sagely as he contradicted her. "No, it isn't. There are women like that. Surely you've heard of them. Millions of them all over the world, dedicated to themselves – the Grand Order of Queen Beeism."

"Rikki!" Karen's protest was half laughter. "How much of this is nonsense? It's quite fascinating, of course, but it's a wee bit implausible."

He crinkled his eyes at her. "You'll learn, kiddo, in time. But I'm glad you're here. You're straight and absolutely direct, and Liane needs a friend. I'm fed up with the deal she's been getting. She's trying so hard to be a carbon copy of Celia and the effect is disastrous, as Celia well knows. The funny thing is Lee could be highly individual once she's thrown off the shackles. Celia doesn't want men staring at her daughter – she might catch some of that gratifying admiration. She actually prefers Liane a mess, so she can steal the show. Vanity, thy name is woman. Hideous, hideous vanity!"

Karen stared at him, completely nonplussed. He winked at her and she began to laugh. Was this purely an act? Rikki always did like to shock.

"You needn't laugh," he said severely, his eyes on her face.

"Rikki, you're being ridiculous. Come on, admit it!"

"Ridiculous?" Karen sat speechless, struck by the inflection he gave the word. "No," Rikki replied, picking his words carefully. "Mothers are sometimes jealous of their own daughters, Karo. It has been known to happen."

Karen looked down at her hands. Despite his words and their implied disloyalty, she felt moved to a quick sympathy. Ever sensitive to people, she sensed in Rikki a long-established hurt he was at pains to conceal with a facetious manner. But she had some experience of the fraudulent heart. Rikki was in his own way suffering.

His bright eyes slipped over her, compelling her attention.

"You know, Karo, with your lovely face and true woman's compassion, I'm crazy about you already. I think we'll get married."

Her face lit up with startled laughter. "You're joking, I hope."

"I'm not, can't you tell by my eyes?" His smile was very sweet, giving her a quick glimpse of the boy he was all those years before. "Don't take me too seriously, Karo. I talk a lot of nonsense. Fundamentally I'm a warm-hearted, affectionate boy with normal instincts. Any slight deviation can be explained or excused by the circumstances of my childhood." He sat back and regarded her. "Now you're something else again. Whatever kind of life you've had, it's made you fearless – those beautiful, clear eyes. I can see right through to your soul. There's nothing twisted there. No plotting and planning . . . the endless conniving."

Karen stood up with some agitation. "If you're trying to intrigue me, Rikki, you're succeeding a little too well. I've a picture of seething discontent. Who's at the bottom of it . . . Guy?" she hazarded.

Rikki looked up in genuine astonishment. "Guy? Good God, no! Why should it be Guy? Guy is as direct as you are. I have a shot at him occasionally, but I could no more bring him down than an eagle. He really is the most extraordinarily vital man. He resembles ordinary human beings like a tractor resembles his own Jaguar. Pure *machismo*, of course."

"Good grief, what's that?" Karen looked startled.

"*Machismo?*" Rikki snorted. "Spanish for a sexy forceful male – the big power game player with just a dash of playboy, and the merest suggestion of ruthlessness all you females seem to go mad for."

"Leave me out of it, please," Karen said repressively.

"Well, all the others, then, doll. They waft through his life trying to make the big impression, then wham! flat on their face."

"I'm not surprised, he reminds me distinctly of one of the Borgias."

Rikki laughed uproariously. "Well, I'm exchanging a scion of the Borgias for a captivating child."

Karen smiled, showing her small, pretty teeth. "I'm honoured, Rikki. When do I get to see your work?"

"When the mood takes me," he grinned conspiratorially. "I'm rather like a new mother at the moment. You know, frightened to let anyone take a peek at the baby in case they don't agree I've produced something wonderful."

There was a quick rush of light footsteps and they both looked towards the door. Patricia Amber came into the room, speaking with gentle vivacity. "Well, Karen, what do you

43

think of Rikki, after all these years?" Her luminous dark eyes circled Karen to Rikki. "Of course, he *is* rather a leg-puller."

Karen smiled. "So I imagine. Do I ever take him seriously?"

"Nearly always," his aunt replied unexpectedly. "Rikki's extremely intuitive, especially where women are concerned."

"And you're a saint, Trish," Rikki grinned irrepressibly. "As a matter of fact I've just been filling in my dear family for Karo's benefit. Pre-warned is pre-armed, so they say."

Patricia Amber's eyes flew to Karen's. "What exactly *has* he been saying, and on your very first day?"

"Just a lightning sketch of the local legend. Nothing too telling," Rikki quipped lightly, and jumped to his feet, obviously bent on changing the subject. "Now what about an aperitif before lunch, then I'll be off to the studio," he said brightly. "I've some wonderful ideas formulating."

His aunt's head veered round to Karen. "Karen, I suppose. She has the kind of bones I imagine a would-be artist would like to capture."

"Exactly," Rikki bowed, "and thank you for the faint praise. Nevertheless, I feel I can appraise my subject without diffidence. Young as she is, Karen's face is touched with a certain sadness, nostalgia perhaps. It has a most poignant effect on beauty."

Karen looked at him strangely. "Guy said almost the same thing."

Rikki winked knowingly. "I'm not surprised. Guy, let me tell you, had you possibly missed it, is highly susceptible to all forms of beauty. I've seen him handling his treasures – the *inanimate* ones, of course. He has a fine eye for beauty." The aquamarine gaze narrowed maliciously. "By the same token, all the animate ones have been tearing their hair out for years . . . The things I could tell you!"

"Please don't, there's a dear. You're not an *enfant terrible* any longer." Patricia Amber spoke with finality. "Now what about that drink . . . a Martini for me, I think. What about you, Karen? Would you prefer something else, a sherry perhaps?"

"No, a Martini would be lovely. Horror of horrors in this household, I don't care much for sherry."

Rikki burst into satirical cackles. "Not even the famous Amber Amontillado." He launched into full-scale advertising blurb. "Spark up your party with Amber Amontillado, and colour your world golden. Let your guests capture the soft full bouquet with the oak astringency showing through. The full 'nutty' aftertaste of Australia's finest dry sherry — Amber Amontillado."

Karen smiled. "I'm sold! I haven't, in fact, ever tried it. I'd better do so now and show the proper respect."

Rikki moved off, still chattering. "But never in a coloured glass, dear child. Always remember it. Never, never the coloured glass. I swear I've seen Guy change colour when presented with champagne in a tinted wine-glass."

"Very proper too. I'm in entire agreement." His aunt smiled at him. "Perhaps I'll have one too, Rikki, and make your day."

"I say, I've timed that nicely!" They all swung round as a tall, very lean man in his seventies, with a silver shock of hair, came into the room holding Philip's hand. "One young man delivered and ready for his lunch."

Philip smiled up at his companion, then sped across the room, putting his arm around Karen. "I've had the most marvellous time, Karo. It's all terrific. You should see it — the vineyards and the cellars. The size of the casks, they're enormous! Uncle Guy has put in the most fantastic refrigeration plant because it's too hot at vintage time, and there are tractors and harvesters and all kinds of mechanical equipment —" Pip broke off for breath, though his admiration continued to effervesce. "I've learnt an awful lot off Uncle Mark, he's terribly clever. He's writing a book about the vine through the ages."

The wistfulness that touched his tone made them all laugh. Mark Amber interrupted the excited flow of chatter.

"And I couldn't have asked for a more intelligent lad to show about the place." He turned to his niece. "I think he has the makings of a true vigneron, Trish." His eyes moved back and sought Karen's. "And this, of course, is Karen." He moved swiftly across the room and took her hand, appraising her with the complete frankness of a child, or those well advanced in years. He took his time, then bent his silvery head, kissing her cheek soundly. "Welcome home, my dearest child. It's been far too long for all of us."

All at once Karen felt the tears coming. She stood there helplessly, feeling as stiff and awkward as a schoolgirl; as if with a gesture Mark Amber had somehow touched the well spring of her emotions.

"Gosh, you're not crying!" Philip burst out in alarm. "Karo never cries." His widened dark eyes circled the others with so much obvious consternation that the moment of tension was broken.

Mark Amber put a comforting arm around Karen's shoulders, causing the ever articulate Rikki to remark on his easy gallantry. He reached up and touched his silver hair. "I'm not as old as the snow on my head would have you think, Rikki. Now shake hands with young Philip here."

They all watched the rather awkward salute between the child and young man, while Mark Amber continued to say, so casually and easily, all the right things. By the time they went in to lunch, the whole party was caught up on a tide of youthful reunion.

The great house was silent. Not a shutter banged nor a floorboard creaked. Karen slipped out of bed and thrust her arms into her robe — an orange winter silk. It was one of her real extravagances, bought especially for Belle Amber, and a wonderful foil for her black hair and gleaming tiptilted eyes. Sleep was impossible. Her mind was just a mad carousel flinging off people and impressions. It had been an emotional day — her headache was proof of it. It was making itself felt by the minute, a dull throb that threatened to stagger her eyes. There were Veganin in the medicine cabinet in the downstairs bathroom.

She had noticed them when Pip was washing his face and hands for dinner. Two would certainly take care of her headache, induce a deep sleep.

Out in the carpeted hallway she moved swiftly as a shadow. Every inch of the house was as familiar to her now as it had been in her childhood. She found her way easily along the top floor with bright moonlight falling in patches through the casement windows. In the fathomless dark well at the base of the stairs she moved without apprehension into an unmoving dark shadow, then her heart lunged with fright and her stifled cry was buried under a lean hand.

"The things one stumbles across in a dark house!"

At the sound of that laughing, mocking voice, Karen nipped at the hand with her small teeth, steadying her voice with an effort.

"You frightened me!"

He laughed softly, his hand moving to the curve of her shoulder.

"Frightened you, Karen? I was beginning to think that quite impossible. Characteristically you're attaching no importance whatever to my quite equal sense of shock. You're not a somnambulist, are you?"

"Of course not. I couldn't sleep . . ." her voice was a mixture of plaintive indignation. "I have a headache," she tacked on, feeling disorientated in the soft darkness with this wildly disturbing man. She rounded on him swiftly. "No one expected you until tomorrow, you know."

His hand encircled her bare wrist. "I come and go as I please, Karen," he laughed, and drew her along with him across the hallway and into the library.

She heard the door shut with a gentle click, then he reached out and flicked at a switch. Light flared golden on the beautifully appointed room, an entire wall of books that would satisfy the most ardent bibliophile, and contemporary furniture of simplicity and quality, club chairs upholstered in leather and heavy handwoven fabric. Karen met the dark waiting eyes, endlessly, endlessly feeling as if she had stumbled into something far more than dazzling light, and she shut her own eyes briefly in sheer self-defence. He was wearing evening clothes with an elegance and splendour that could not be denied. She couldn't bear to look at him, certainly not give him the satisfaction of judging her spontaneous reactions.

His smothered laugh moved the silky dark hair at her temples. "You can't change things by shutting your eyes and wishing, Karen."

Her eyes flew open again, meeting his, amused, beneath quirking brows.

"I can try," she murmured hardily, conveying with her voice that she was in no mood to be trifled with. But she trembled as his eyes slipped over her face, touched her slender throat, moved over the subtle contours of her body.

Without moving he asked levelly, "Why do you distrust me, Karen?"

Conflict was hovering now between them with an almost compulsive fascination.

"You can't wash out the past," she said carefully, "pretend it hasn't happened."

He looked away from the accusation in her great golden eyes.

"That's very profound of you, Karen," he said sardonically, and moved over to the far end of the room; at the flick of his wrist a section of panelling opened to reveal hi-fidelity equipment, a television, and a full-scale bar. He had his broad back to her. "Tell me more. I'm always interested in the extent and depth of a young woman's observations." He drew out an exquisite crystal decanter and two matching tumblers, turning to smile slightly into her ominous eyes. "Don't look at me like that, little one. I'm not about to ply you with liquor, then sell you down the river . . . or worse."

She coloured at the mockery in his voice and lowered her eyes, feeling hopelessly out of her depth. The silence spun out until he drawled lazily, "You're an ornamental child, aren't you?" He walked over the smooth expanse of buff carpet and held out a watered-down whisky. "Drink that down. It will help you sleep ... shift that headache." She stood unmoving and he thrust it towards her. "Do take it, child."

She took it then, tipping her head with a show of spirit.

"Please don't 'child' me, Guy. I don't care to be used for target practice."

He gave a soft mocking laugh. "My dear Karen, I'm handling you with kid gloves, if you only knew it. Up-to-date, temperamental young women and my kind of life have been mutually exclusive. You'll have to forgive me if I'm a little slow in getting the hang of you.'

She hesitated, looking uncertainly at the deep golden liquid in her glass.

"Drink it, my restless butterfly. It's guaranteed to be harmless in that quantity."

Karen took a tentative sip, surprising herself by liking it, then took another sip while he glanced at his watch.

"I'd better say goodnight," she murmured hastily, feeling an intruder.

"It's morning, little one, but why worry? You said you couldn't sleep."

"But surely you need your sleep," she countered, anxious to remove herself from the circle of his compelling charm. "Though they tell me you're a human dynamo."

He smiled slightly. "I've managed on very little sleep for a long time now, Karen. But your consideration does you credit. Sit down and tell me what you've been doing."

She sank into a tan leather club chair, her gown parting over long slender legs and showing the lacy tip of her nightgown. She drew it together swiftly, biting on her lip, furious with herself for feeling so gauche.

His smile was maddening. "You shouldn't feel so ill at ease with a relative, Karen."

"Relative to your attitude to women, I don't see why not," she flared uncontrollably. "You make me at least feel like a display piece under the eye of an exacting connoisseur!"

He threw off the contents of his glass with a laugh.

"You'd pass the test any day, Karen. Which brings me to a certain matter I meant to discuss with you. You never cashed that cheque I sent you for clothes. You'll need a fairly extensive wardrobe here. We do a great deal of entertaining, but I'd hardly expect you to have earned enough in your short career to cover every exigency."

She tried to control her mounting colour. "My wardrobe is adequate," she countered repressively, feeling as absurdly prim as a milkmaid. He must have thought so too, for his mouth twitched.

"How easily you fire, little one. Are you always so prickly? You look as though you should be as soft as that silk." His eyes flickered over the orange robe. "Which, incidentally, is the only thing I've seen you in that suits you."

Karen sat up straighter. "Thank you, I must be thankful for that!"

He ignored her sarcasm. "What about the party on Sunday? Have you anything suitable for that? The women in our social circle usually dress to the eyes. Celia must spend a fortune on clothes."

"Lucky Celia," Karen said dryly. "But I really can't imagine *my* life reduced to the sole consideration of the right clothes, the right hair-do, the right make-up." She sketched a rapid gesture with her hand. "It's quite incomprehensible to me."

"It is now, my little cat. Ah well, being a true beauty you might carry the night." He was smiling faintly, thoughtfully.

Her slender shoulders moved. "I won't disgrace you at any rate, even if I don't exactly measure up to the exalted company.

"Then you refuse my offer?"

"I do." Her hand went to her temple, then pushed back the

50

heavy fall of hair that swept her shoulder. "Do you know, I feel quite ethereal," she murmured inconsequently.

"The effect of the whisky," he smiled. "How's the headache?"

"Magically it's gone." Her admission was tinged with faint reluctance.

He had to smile. "You hate to admit any good coming from our encounters, don't you? You betray yourself with every look, every gesture." He came across to her, swiftly drawing her to her feet. She swayed slightly and he kept a steadying hand on her shoulder, running a caressing thumb over her collar bone. "Today has been too much for you. You're an emotional child. I shouldn't really fence with you, but it's proving irresistible."

"Such a change from your usual sophisticated style?" She looked up at him, unable to subdue the mischief in her eyes.

He shook her gently. "Your name should be Kate, not Karen. You'll never get a husband with that ever-ready backchat."

"But I don't *want* a husband," she managed, feeling suddenly sleepy.

"What you want won't have much to do with it, I'm afraid." He shook her again. "Come on now, Karen, call it a night. You're out on your feet."

He turned her about with gentle force, and a long skein of her hair fell over his sleeve. He curled it around his hand experimentally, then tucked it behind her ear, looking down at her lazily. "What tiny ears you have, Karen. Almost no lobe to them. I must remember never to buy you earrings."

She looked back at him with wide, startled eyes.

"You must remember never to buy me *anything*."

"I'm afraid I won't be able to keep to that, Karen. Dressing you, for one thing, would prove quite rewarding."

"I'll manage on my own!"

"Very virtuous, little one. In the days gone by you would undoubtedly have carried a banner."

"And you would have had me in chains," she countered, then

laughed aloud. "This is getting us nowhere, as usual." She blinked back at him with sleepy exhaustion.

"Where exactly do you want to go?"

"To bed, of course," she retorted, mildly astonished, then fled at the glittering undercurrent in his eyes.

CHAPTER III

Guy and Patricia drove into town early next morning for the monthly board meeting, leaving Karen the run of the house. Philip, with a few more days of freedom before settling into his new school, was up with the sun, caught up, at ten, in the mystique of the vine. There was so much to see, so much to learn, and Uncle Mark had promised to let him ride up to the front gate on one of the bulk wine tankers.

Karen, listening to his excited chatter at breakfast time, felt quite proud of him. It was amazing what a receptive young mind could store away in such a short space of time! To their mutual satisfaction he was able to reel off the varietal names of the grapes used to make different types of wines, both red and white, and Uncle Mark, as an added incentive had promised to take him over their Lagonda Vale estate, forty miles to the north-east, and famous for its "rieslings".

In the post-breakfast quiet, Karen spent a little time tidying her room. She put her things away with a feeling of pleasure, taking time off to enjoy her surroundings. In style, her own room offered a departure from the rest of the house, for the décor was unashamedly contemporary: the tailored bedspread, the two deep armchairs, the window wall and the drapes were covered in a ravishing print of rust, gold and orange and the desk and low wall cabinets on either side of the bed, were handsome contemporary pieces that matched the dark stained shutters over windows that looked out over the pool garden.

Even the small adjoining bathroom had a distinct personality, decorated in the same striking colour scheme with an elegant eye to finish and detail. There was not the slightest doubt it had been furnished with love, specifically with Karen in mind.

Downstairs again, in the living room, she opened up the Steinway and struck a tentative chord. It reverberated in the silence, signalling her urgent desire to practise in earnest. The high ceiling and heavy carpeting would cut a lot of the piano's big tone. Besides, she wouldn't be disturbing anyone. It was all of three weeks since she last had the opportunity to play. She sat down at the keyboard and ran off a few determined arpeggios. That was the end of it!

The old deeply familiar sensation of power and pleasure rushed over her and she settled herself on to the long piano seat and began with Tausig – technical work vastly rewarding to the performer but sheer torture to anyone obliged to listen for long periods. Three-quarters of an hour flew past while she practised on, her forehead faintly pleated with concentration. These were virtuoso exercises and they required her full attention.

Rikki's voice at the doorway startled her very thoroughly.

"Just one more arpeggio and so help me I'll go out of my mind!"

Karen swung round to encounter his magnificent scowl.

"I'm sorry, Rikki. Did I disturb you?"

"Of course you did, moronic girl. Why else would I be here?" Just as suddenly he relented, gathering his persuasive powers. "I suppose all technical work is a bind, but seriously, Karo, what about sitting for me this afternoon?"

"I'd like that, Rikki. What time?"

"About two-ish." His eyes narrowed. "You know, Karo, I'm getting cardiac complications just looking at you. You have the sort of face the knights of old would joust about."

"Jest about?" she quipped lightly.

He ignored her facetiousness, completely serious in his appraisal. "I'm not sure how I'll go about this. Your face is the most intriguing mixture of hauteur and mischief."

"Good lord!" Karen laughed in earnest.

"Forgive me for being super-literal, dear girl, it's the artist

54

in me," Rikki drawled sarcastically.

"And it's irresistible." Karen's eyes gleamed through their dark lashes. Rikki did take himself seriously!

"If any other girl but you said that, I should bolt!"

"Then why don't you? I'm going to finish my practice."

Rikki took this piece of information badly. He struck his brow. "God give me strength!"

Karen sat for a moment swinging her legs, then she drifted into an exquisite Liszt Consolation. That at least should soothe Rikki's nerves.

It did! His gilded head appeared momentarily around the door. "Now why didn't you tell me you played like an angel?"

Chopin Études followed the Liszt, then Falla, Ravel and Debussy. It was the greatest pleasure to Karen, doubly so after the few silent weeks without her piano.

Mark Amber, coming into the house in search of her, made for the living room with an expression of delighted surprise. He was in the room several moments before Karen became aware of his presence. She spun around quickly.

"Back so soon, Uncle Mark?"

"I'd have come back sooner, had I known there was going to be a recital. Pip and I wanted you to join us, but now I think I'll just stay here." He moved over to an armchair, his silvery shock of hair coming to rest against the high back. "Now why can't all women play the piano? It's such a wonderful accomplishment and yet it's so sadly out of fashion. In my day every young lady was expected to have some degree of proficiency, but I can't say I remember anyone playing half so beautifully as you, Karen."

She smiled at the genuine ring of sincerity in his voice.

"I suspect you're a charmer, Uncle Mark."

"Well, I do have a favourite piece," he smiled, not displeased by her compliment. "Schumann's *Devotion*. Do you know it? I heard Horowitz play it many years ago as an encore at one of his New York concerts, and I've never forgotten it."

Karen's left hand found the chord of A flat. "I'm no Horowitz, Uncle Mark, but if you close your eyes tightly it won't be so noticeable."

He smiled and made the gesture of shutting his eyes, only to open them a few seconds later. The combined visual and auditory effect was quite entrancing to him. Young Karen was a born musician, with a special affinity for the piano, like her father before her. When the last note died away he conveyed his great pleasure by nodding his head vigorously. He had no wish to shatter the spell by speaking. Karen smiled her fingers seeking out another lovely old melody – Liszt's *Liebestraum*. The gentle "Ah!" from behind her told her she had guessed correctly. It too was a favourite!

But the reign of contentment was to be broken! Philip's dark head came round the living room door, tilted like a robin's. "Gosh, Uncle Mark, is this where you are? I've been hard on your trail for a quarter of an hour. You're not going to sit there and listen to Karen, are you? She can play for you any time."

Mark Amber came out of his absorption, and stood up imperturbably. "I'm afraid Pip has the prior claim, Karen, but your next recital can't come soon enough. Thank you, my dear. Now what about joining us on our tour of inspection?" He walked over to help her close down the leaf of the piano, then led both young people out into the spring sunshine.

Morning was brilliantly blue and golden and a profusion of spring flowers greeted them everywhere. Flynn, the head gardener, was an authority on the rhododendron genus and the two varieties seemed to spill over everywhere: the paper-thin azaleas, masses upon masses of them, in delicately petalled profusion, breaking up long vistas of greensward, or nestling in great pink and white drifts under the arched branches of the beautiful old scribbly gums fringed by the crimson ruffled trusses of the "true" rhododendron. Unexpected little gardens appeared behind ledges of boxwood and masses of succulents flourished in a bewildering number of varieties around the pond at the foot of the embankment.

By the time they reached the vineyards, Karen felt a great surge of happiness. They moved slowly over the sloping gravelly ground, walking the dead straight rows of luxuriant vines.

"Vitis vinifera!" Philip chanted happily, running on before them.

Mark Amber smiled into Karen's amused eyes. "The sacred vine! The symbol of both pagan and christian deities from our earliest times."

"Incredible, isn't it, the aura that surrounds it. Yet it's the sturdiest of plants! You're writing a book about it, aren't you, Uncle Mark?"

"I've *been* writing it, on and off, for the past twenty years."

"That's a long time!" Karen looked up at his clear-cut profile. He was extraordinarily vital for a man of his years.

"There's quite a lot of ground to cover, Karen, when you consider that the vine's origins are lost in the mists of antiquity. Why, some authorities put its beginnings as early as 8000 B.C. At any rate, we can be sure the vine was established in the Tigris-Euphrates valleys before 4000 B.C. You might be interested to know the very first reference to a vineyard occurs in the earliest work of literature there is — the Epic of Gilgamesh."

"I must confess my ignorance!" Karen smiled, and stopped to remove a pebble from her open sandal.

"A poem in the Semitic language, my dear," Mark Amber steadied her, "written on earthenware and thus preserved forever." He began to recite in a soft, rhythmic undertone:

"Amethyst it bore as its fruit;
Grapevine was trellised, good to behold;
Lapis lazuli it wore as grape clusters;
Fruit it bore magnificent to look upon."

"Lapis lazuli! what a beautiful word!" Karen watched him as he bent to cradle a green cluster of berries in his hand.

"By the time Homer wrote the Iliad, wine was not only the ordinary drink of the Greeks but regarded as one of the country's finest natural products. From Greece to Rome and with Caesar's conquest of Gaul to the great home of the vine – *la belle* France! I can't imagine any wine-lover being without the great vintages of Bordeaux, Burgundy or the Loire, not to mention Champagne." He straightened up to smile at her. "One day soon, my dear, I hope you have the great pleasure of finding yourself in Paris with sufficient money and leisure to enjoy some of the great French wines. On a day like today, when the weather is sparkling, I think I would order champagne ... Veuve Cliquot, or Pol Roget perhaps ... the great classic champagnes. They lend such enchantment to an occasion." He gave her a wicked, sidelong look. "Actually, Karen, you won't have to go quite so far as Paris, Guy laid in quite a stock up at the house. I'll get him to open a few bottles on Saturday, though we usually boost our own products at parties." He laughed softly.

"I'm longing to see Aunt Celia and Liane again. I hope they'll be home in time for it."

"Almost certainly, my dear." Mark Amber's voice was rather dry. He leaned towards her, serious, confidential. "You might not recognise your Aunt Celia, Karen. She's changed a great deal in the past few years."

"May I be permitted to ask in what way?" she asked gravely.

"It would be too difficult to define once you got past the obvious. Richard's death was a great tragedy for all of us, but more so for Celia. She lost her sheet anchor when she lost Richard. He knew how to keep her in hand, satisfy the woman in her. Some women need ... *demand,* even, a man's constant regard."

"Is she unhappy, then, Uncle Mark?"

His surprise at this was genuine. "No, I wouldn't say *Celia* was unhappy, my dear."

Her hand moved a little helplessly. "Rikki seems a little . . . lost?"

He considered the word gravely. "Perhaps, but Rikki will make out. It's Liane I'm concerned about. She's very much affected by her mother's attitudes. They're so different in type, yet Liane tries so hard to emulate her mother. Natural enough, of course. I must say Celia is a great credit to us. She's charming and witty and a delight to look upon – far more so at close on – forty, let me whisper it, than she ever was as a girl, proving indisputably that youth is not necessarily the time of a woman's greatest glamour. Her youthful prettiness has gained a powerful new dimension, I can tell you. Yes," he added reflectively, "Celia is a wonderful piece of artifice."

Karen gave a trill of rising laughter. "That sounds rather acid, Uncle Mark. Surely it wasn't intended?"

He answered her smile, not at all shamefaced. "Perhaps I'd better rephrase it. Celia is a work of art!"

Her smile exonerated him. "I must admit I'm looking forward to seeing her again."

His dark eyes were intent in their steadiness. "You sound positively intrigued. Who's been talking?"

"Why, no one. What could you mean?" She widened her eyes at him innocently. "It's a wonder Aunt Celia hasn't married again, isn't it?"

His glance met hers, briefly and she thought a trifle warily. "Perhaps she's waiting for a man like Richard." He took her arm. "You know, Karen, we used to have a little kitten with eyes like yours . . . and it was just as inquisitive."

"Do you mean to reprove me, Uncle Mark?" She smiled up at him, her head tilted.

"No, my dear, but you're too damned observant and I'm not going to say too much. Now, to get back to a safe topic. We have some new plantings further on . . . more Cabernet. Come and see them. We won't let Pip get too far ahead of us. He might run under the sprays."

And so Mark Amber redirected Karen's attention gently but firmly. To mention the "new" Celia Amber was to tread on very dangerous ground indeed!

It was well after lunch before Karen found her way to Rikki's studio, over the garage. She paused outside the door, then rapped smartly. Rikki's tall, slender figure loomed up at the door, one errant lock falling over his brow in the traditional Bohemian-Beatnik fashion.

"Are you from the police?" he asked truculently, taking up a position.

"Why, are you on the run?"

He surveyed her closely. "Pushing marijuana, then?"

"Not the type!" Karen peered under his arm at the superbly equipped studio. No artist's garret this!

"Well then, is it possible to hold a serious discussion with you?" Rikki persisted, still blocking the door.

"Never about art." Somehow Karen struck on the right password and Riki relented and pressed her shoulder.

"Come in. If there's one person I hate it's a self-confessed expert." He followed her in and waved a hand towards a stack of canvases. "Take a look, childhood chum, and enjoy an uninformed laugh."

She walked towards the canvases with an expression of interest."

"I hope you don't expect tact and consideration," she flung over her shoulder, herself well versed in receiving constructive criticism.

Rikki quirked his brow at her. "Fire away without fear of displeasure!"

Karen went straight to her task, feeling Rikki's eyes watching her. He seemed nervous yet anxious to have her opinion, however unqualified. She examined canvas after canvas, then pulled one out and left it propped up against the wall. It was a very fine picture, she thought; a landscape of hills and vine-yards and a sky full of scudding clouds – the sky as she had seen today! The style wasn't abstract, yet it wasn't slavishly literal either. It was glowing and imaginative and seemed to radiate that authority inherent in any work of art.

Karen forgot Rikki, forgot everything. She pulled out another, studying it and setting it down.

"I'm experimenting a bit, now," Rikki explained almost apologetically, clearing his throat.

Karen turned towards him, her topaz eyes gleaming. "I'm no expert, Rikki, but I do think I have an instinctive eye for such things." She hesitated for a moment. "What I'm trying to say is, I think you're very good indeed. I never expected any-thing like this. Everything you do seems to work together – colour, form, planes, all perfectly related. I love everything here, especially that landscape. It's so deeply familiar, yet you've handled it with so much freshness and verve. I can almost see the grapes ripening."

"You can?" Rikki looked back at her with a kind of be-wilderment. "Sometimes I think I'm well on my way to ex-pressing myself. Things are so different these days, even the method of handling the paint. My teacher used to say that I showed a great deal of promise, but Celia said that was because we are – who we are, if you know what I mean. The Ambers and all that. It pays to keep in with them." He swung off the subject. "I don't go in for anything detailed, you might have noticed, Karo. I try to lead the eye gently from plane to plane, colour mass to colour mass." He grinned suddenly. "I hope I'm succeeding. Anyway, don't let me get started on my hobby-horse."

"Why ever not? As an artist you're entitled to. Really, Rikki, I had no idea!" Karen's eyes roamed over the light-filled studio. "This is super-equipped, isn't it? I thought you might not be able to live up to the part. But you're the genuine article. I'll be honoured to sit for you, Rikki. In the years to come I'll be able to boast, Richard Amber painted my portrait before he became famous!"

She felt a rising excitement. "How come the family haven't encouraged you? Wouldn't you like to continue your studies overseas? It would be a marvellous experience for you. Mastering new techniques; the stimulating companionship of your own kind . . . to learn from . . . to talk to."

"Karo, sweetheart, you've brushed me with angel's wings!" Rikki lifted her hand to his mouth and kissed it. "None of the family, with the exception of Celia and occasionally Liane, whose artistic soul is lodged in her stomach, have seen any of these latter canvases. Up until about six months ago I was working my way out of a morass. You know, trying freakish experiments. Guy, I think, sees me as a mummy's darling, sheltered and cherished, a pampered pet, weakened by indulgence. I've done nothing to dispel the idea. Aunt Trish, of course, never intrudes on my privacy. She makes a point of not interfering, so I don't think she knows what to make of it all, what with Celia and hints of a dithering dilettante son."

"Is that what your mother really thinks?"

Rikki's voice was strained. "I don't really know, Karo. I don't think she has any great opinion of my work, and unlike you, my pet, she's well informed on the subject. That's what worries me. You must admit she's set me up well. This is an expensive setting for the boy genius."

Karen's great topaz eyes were fixed on him with mingled scepticism and fascination. Celia was sounding more complex by the minute. She couldn't reconcile this new updated version with the pretty pink and white figurine of her childhood.

Rikki looked up and intercepted her gaze.

"Hold it!" He jumped up enthusiastically. "Sit over there . . . in that chair. That's it. Relax. The muse has descended upon me. I'll just fill in some structural lines. I can't even visualise the finished effect. This is only a first laying in of the skeleton, as it were." He was rattling on excitedly, preparing his palette, wiping paint on his already psychedelic pants. "I promise you, you'll be satisfied with whatever result!"

The lovely gaiety touched Karen's mouth. "I'm quite sure of it, Rikki." She smiled into his eyes, now as brilliant as any aquamarines.

He searched amid the jumble of tubes of paint, rags and brushes, found what he wanted, then busied himself squeezing liberal quantities of pigments on to his palette. He glanced up at Karen, his expression preoccupied.

"Turn your left profile just a little ... that's it! Now right shoulder back ... back ... Heavens, no!" he came toward her, frowning. "I don't want you to strike attitudes. That's better! ... relax." He patted the offending shoulder.

Karen tried not to laugh. Rikki couldn't be more intent if he was a much lauded academist. She sat back feeling faintly fatigued. Rikki swept in the structural lines while Karen let her thoughts roam further afield. Half an hour passed, the silence unbroken except for Rikki's intermittent comments on the phases through which the portrait could be expected to pass.

He was in deadly earnest and clearly not disposed towards receiving humorous suggestions from her. Despite herself, Karen, who could never take herself very seriously, was impressed as most people are in the presence of genuine dedication. They both jumped a little at a loud knock on the door. A girl put her head around it, with what to Karen was a vaguely heart-breaking smile.

"I'm home!" she announced blithely. "Idiotic thing to say, I know, but it's all I can think of."

Karen jumped up, smiling. "Liane!" She made towards the other girl's outstretched hands.

Rikki beat his brow. "No hope of getting my model to pose for me." His tone was mournful, but there was an under-current of something like elation in his voice.

"But I will, of course," Karen flung back over her shoulder.

"The unselfish, beautiful spirit which is yours!" He looked over at his sister. "Come in, Lee. For God's sake don't hover." His sister pulled a face at him, not at all put out by his aggressive style. The two girls embraced with unfeigned pleasure in their meeting. Liane, much the taller, drew back a little, a wry smile on her mouth.

"You look lovely, Karo. And so nice! I was afraid you'd be madly superior or something. Guy said you were as beautiful as an orchid." She brushed a well kept hand over her head. "I look a mess, I bet!"

"And now you're just angling for a compliment," Karen smiled back at her, not quite believing in Guy's exotic description.

"She's not, God help her, but it's a nice change, I'll admit." Rikki ran a paint-smeared hand over his pants.

Liane stood in the centre of the room, very tall, slim and long-legged with a slouch that undoubtedly meant she was distressed by her height. She had good features, far better than average eyes, large and darkly lustrous, but somehow she failed to measure up to her potential. Her outfit was beautiful and obviously expensive and it should have suited her, but it didn't. Just as the short bubble of dark curls formed an entirely wrong frame for her well-defined face.

Karen leaned back against a bench beside Rikki. "I can't get over it, Lee. Just a few short years, yet you've grown up in the interval."

"Grown and grown and grown! You're disappointed, I can tell." Liane gave a small grin, gazing amiably at her brother. "As far as looks go, Rikki grabbed the lot!"

"Oh, for heaven's sake, don't keep knocking yourself, girl. There are always enough people around to do that. Where's Celia?" Rikki tacked on pretty tersely.

Liane's eyes flickered. "She has a few more engagements in town and she wanted me to come on ahead. Colin will bring her down on Saturday evening."

"Colin is the fiancé," Rikki explained, and rolled his eyes at Karen.

"My very best wishes, Liane. I was forgetting – a soignée young woman *and* engaged! I can't wait to meet Colin."

Rikki groaned, but Liane took no notice of him. She gave a very white smile. Her teeth were beautiful and so was her smile. For an instant she looked very much like her Aunt Patricia, but unlike her aunt she had yet to develop a distinctive style. A different hair-do would make all the difference, Karen decided, her eyes narrowing unconsciously. Liane simply wasn't curls! It was a wonder she didn't realise it.

"Colin's a dream!" Liane was rhapsodising. "He's clever and attractive. He's in the P.R. section of the firm." Prosaic as the words were they held some magic for Liane, for her eyes were melting with love. "I really don't know what he sees in me!"

Rikki exploded, rounding on his sister with great irritation. "Turn it up, Lee! You don't know what he sees in you. Have a heart! All this half-humorous self-deprecation makes my teeth ache."

"But you're a good-looking girl, Lee," Karen broke in hastily, catching sight of Rikki's face. He appeared to be working himself into a mild frenzy. He was undoubtedly a volatile young man, but just as clearly devoted to his sister.

Liane had her eyes fixed on Karen with a look of incredulity. "You can't *mean* it!"

"Good grief, I wouldn't *say* it if I didn't *mean* it." Even Karen sounded faintly irritated, and Rikki grinned. "I see you a little differently, perhaps. I always liked your hair as you used to wear it, straight and shiny with a deep fringe."

"Like I did as a child?" Liane almost squeaked.

"Well, the style could be modified. It gave you distinction. You have the Amber features," Karen pointed out.

"And the Amber height! What an almighty handicap," Liane lamented.

"She wants to be little!" Rikki said with soft vehemence. "Can you beat it! A tiny little thing like Celia." His voice picked up suddenly. "I reckon any girl worth her salt would want to sit tall in the saddle."

Karen burst out laughing. "That's a funny way to put it!" Her eyes questioned Liane's. "Tell me about Colin."

"Not here, she won't." Rikki straightened up with an air of absolute finality.

"He means it," Liane laughed.

"I'll say I do! Can't you see the lunatic light in my eye?" Rikki advanced on his sister and just as suddenly put his arms around her, hugging her to him. "Try to get the Big View of everything, kiddo. Run along now, and talk girl talk with Karen. She'll be a friend to you, if anyone will."

"Thank you for the kind words," Karen smiled, and moved over to Liane. "Come on, Lee, leave the boy genius to it."

"Same time tomorrow?" Rikki came after them and kissed Karen under the ear.

"Same time tomorrow," she agreed, and intercepted Liane's surprised but affectionate glance.

Saturday morning started off unexpectedly. Karen and Liane were just putting the final touches to the flowers when a delivery van swept up the drive. After a cursory glance Karen took no further notice of it. Aunt Patricia was somewhere on the terrace supervising the placing of tubs of flowering azaleas. She would attend to it. A few minutes later Karen heard her name being called. She went out on to the terrace with only a brief startled glance at Liane.

"Yes, Aunt Patricia."

"For you, dear – every last box. I'll get Flynn to put them in the service lift for you."

Karen looked down at the mountain of lilac and gold striped boxes with the flamboyant signature – Regina Gold.

"For me?" she asked inanely.

"Guy's doing, dear. I had an idea he was thinking of something like this ever since he asked me if you were size twelve." Patricia Amber laughed delightedly, the shallow dimple at the corner of her mouth flicking in and out.

"But I can't possibly accept them!"

"Go on with you!" the older woman patted her arm and waved a hand at Flynn who was wheeling a barrow full of plants from the greenhouse. "Oh, Flynn, would you mind giving us a hand here?"

He put down the barrow and walked towards them smiling, a wiry little man with a passion for all things growing.

Karen smiled a greeting, then turned uncertainly towards the house. "I'll just go and check up with Guy." Her throat felt surprisingly dry.

"He's in his study, dear," Patricia Amber called after her, and turned away smiling.

In the house Liane's "Lucky devil!" further unnerved Karen. She walked through to the study and knocked on the door.

"Come in!"

She swallowed on the obstruction in her throat, and opened the door with an air of decision. Guy had his broad back to her, as he took a file out of a cabinet.

"Come into my parlour, said the spider to the fly. Well, what is it, Karo?"

"I think you know very well."

"You do sound severe!" He turned then, with a smile, and faced her, handsome and relaxed in sand-coloured slacks and a matching sweater.

Her eyes rejected his stunning physical elegance. His mouth twitched. "Regina's done her stuff, is that it?"

"The clothes have arrived ... yes," she murmured repressively.

"You know, Karo, you sound positively formidable, and for such a young girl! Tell me, do you want me to deduct the cost of them from your allowance?"

"Don't try to make a fool of me, Guy. You know I couldn't possibly afford a Regina Gold handkerchief, let alone an entire wardrobe."

"Why, have you looked at them?" His dark eyebrows shot up.

"No!"

"Then what are you on about? As it happens they're all genuine reductions at near bargain basement prices, a special on all X.S.S.W.s this month."

"Please don't evade the issue." She tilted her chin at him.

"What *is* the issue, exactly?" An amused glint leapt into his dark eyes.

"Simply this. I can't have you buying my clothes, Guy."

"Why ever not?" He sounded genuinely startled. "What *is* this extraordinary masque of yours, Karen? You don't really believe Heaven will provide for you, do you?" He gave her an odd sidelong smile. "Why won't you allow me to substitute?"

Her expression was young, very haughty. "It's out of the question!"

He came around the desk, with a vital swinging movement. One look at those black, slanting brows and high cheekbones and Karen retreated, coming to rest against the door. The gleam in his eyes, so full of urgency, had a near-hypnotic effect on her, and she over-reacted.

"Don't come near me, you devil!" she burst out, sounding like a scared, inexperienced schoolgirl.

He stopped in his tracks and gave a shout of laughter.

"Good God! I've never in my life been at this sort of disadvantage." He put the back of his hand between his eyes. "Tell me, do you do it on purpose, all these missish manoeuvres? I don't think I've ever encountered a more suspicious young woman. It's quite unnerving!" His eyes travelled over her face and bare throat, conveying to her wary eyes the impression that he was about to launch some bold campaign.

"I'm sorry, but that's the way it is," she announced breathlessly.

"A life and death decision." He was definitely laughing and she had the irritating suspicion that there was more colour in her face and throat than was necessary.

"I go my own way," she added for good measure.

"Strong words, Karen." He turned away from her. "But for all that, you've restored my faith in the eternal ingénue."

"How nice!" Anger brewed up in her at his bantering tone.

"Sarcasm, little one." His eyes rested on her with cool male speculation. "You want to look, you'd love to touch, but you just wouldn't dare," he drawled lightly.

"You'd dare anything," she corrected him, in a voice she did not altogether recognise as her own. "Forgive me for taking up your time."

He closed the gap between them, towering over her.

"Karen, my angel, you've just given way to the unbelievably feminine urge to have the last word." There was a distinct, too distinct edge to his voice. "Run along now, or I just might weaken and wring your lovely neck."

She gave a small shocked exclamation.

"Run along," he repeated, quite equably.

She gave him an almost frighteningly intense look, her topaz eyes shimmering, the pupils dilated.

He looked at her quickly. "No tears of remorse, you unpredictable child?"

She was silent a moment, trying to find her voice. "Hardly," she lied. "I don't in the least regret appearing ungracious."

"Not another word, little cat," he said softly, a dangerous gleam in his eyes. "One can resist one's impulses for only so long."

"I could stay and call your bluff," she managed, refusing to be intimidated.

"In that case I have no other choice." His hand closed over her shoulder and tightened experimentally.

In a frenzy of haste Karen broke away from him and opened the door and slammed it behind her. She was treachously near to tears; the tears of anger more than anything else. These exchanges with Guy absolutely exhausted her, yet she was determined he wouldn't get his own way!

CHAPTER IV

KAREN prepared for the evening with rising excitement. There was some magic in the word "party" that could never be lost. Stoically, she refused to glance in the wardrobe at the rows of mouth-watering creations bearing the Melbourne couturière's label. It was a definite temptation to pull out one of them – the autumn leaf chiffon – but she braced herself to resist it. It would be an out-and-out admission of defeat. Hadn't she sworn she would manage alone?

She moved over to the dressing table, picking things up and putting them down. Her mind really wasn't on anything. If only she *owned* the chiffon she would look rather special. At least once in her life she was entitled to look rather special. Well, wasn't she? She fought a brief, losing battle with the perverse feminine streak that couldn't resist beautiful clothes. She went to the wardrobe and took out the long evening gown, then held it up against her, twirling idly, studying her reflection.

Her eyes picked up the colour of the gown in the most entrancing fashion. She might have known they would. *He* certainly must have known, thus toppling her scruples. She swayed backwards and forwards, feeling dreamy and romantic. This is the real *me*, she thought blissfully. But it was all wishful thinking! She must be strong.

With commendable self-discipline she hung the gown back in the wardrobe, reaching for her only legitimate evening gown – a white moiré taffeta. She had worn it first and last at St. Hilda's annual prizegiving. It looked like an annual prizegiving, she decided with a flash of irritation. Ah well, there was nothing really wrong with it, if you didn't move in the exclusive Amber circles.

She ran her bath, sniffing the fragrance of expensive soap

and bath salts. Aunt Patricia had supplied her with a liberal stock of both, so at least she would smell the part. Dressed in the white taffeta, her dark hair brushed and brushed again into a shining bell, she looked what she was, a beautiful young girl in a simple gown, very likely her first. Which, of course, it was! She hesitated, then wound her mother's pearls around her throat in an effort to reduce the excessive simplicity. She stood back to observe the final effect, then turned down her mouth, thoroughly dissatisfied. Perhaps Aunt Patricia would give the final verdict! Not that anyone would be looking at her with so many established society beauties present.

Crossing over to the central wing, she saw Guy Amber coming up from the cellar. She spun back under the stairs, but it was too late. His arrogant brows shot up as he caught sight of her, then he came towards her purposefully.

"Great God, what are you supposed to be? A refugee from a school concert?"

She tilted her head, her eyes beginning to sparkle. "Untrue and unkind. I think I look rather sweet — simple, unpretentious and quite sweet."

His eyes gave her a critical, head-to-toe appraisal. "My dear Karen, *sweet and simple* is the one thing you're not! But the dress is definitely unpretentious. In fact, not to put too fine a point on it, it's quite dreadful."

"Thank you. I knew I could look to you for approval." She backed away from him, but he took hold of her wrist, compelling her back the way she had come.

"Perhaps you'll tell me what you're doing?" Her skirt flared out as she tried to keep up with him. "I might add you've got my arm in a vice."

Guy's hold loosened a little and he observed her shining dark head, the flawless curve of her cheek. "I'm simply giving you the chance to do yourself justice, Karen."

"To do *you* justice, don't you mean?"

"If you prefer it, though it could be the same thing!" He

moved swiftly along the long corridor until they came to her room. He opened the door and gave her a gentle push through it. Karen stood there, defenceless, in the centre of the rust-coloured carpet, her eyes widening.

"Surely you don't intend to give me personal supervision?"

"How else would I know what you're up to?" He walked across to the huge walk-in wardrobe and riffled through the rows of dresses. "Whether it makes you happy or not," he announced, his voice faintly muffled, "I intend to follow this thing through. I can't have you gumming up with the works with your foolish pride."

"My foolish pride?" she echoed blankly, and refused to look at him.

"This one!" He came back towards her, flicking her averted cheek. "Go try it on, if you haven't already. I'm damn sure you're woman enough to want to look beautiful."

"As long as you think the dress will accomplish it."

He ignored her sarcasm, intent on the colour that crept under her matt ivory skin.

"It will!"

She whisked away from him then and walked into the wardrobe, shutting the long mirrored door with a gesture of wiping her hands of the whole affair. Inside the room, the white moiré taffeta slipped unheeded to the floor. So it was dreadful, was it? she fumed impotently. It wasn't *that* dreadful! In fact it wasn't dreadful at all Several of her pupils had told her they loved it! She stepped into the beautiful swirling chiffon, refusing at first to acknowledge the transformation, then stared back at the vision in the mirror, trying ineffectually, now the moment of truth was upon her, to adjust the deep V of the tiny draped bodice. She had never in her life ventured to show so much of her milky white skin. But at least it wasn't indecent! There simply wasn't enough of her!

She pushed open the wardrobe door, speaking very rapidly to cover her confusion.

"You'll have to fix the rest of the zipper, I can go only so far." She presented her smooth ivory back to him and he made the necessary adjustment with one precise movement, his hands moving to rest briefly on her narrow waist. She met his eyes in their mirrored reflection and her heart leapt in her breast to thump erratically on.

Physical attraction was a snare, a delusion. They had no real basis for friendship. In fact they were gliding over the thin ice of antagonism. She kept her voice bantering, though it cost her an effort.

"I feel rather like Lucrezia Borgia dressed for an assignment! Are you sure there isn't some business acquaintance you want fascinated? You know, use my feminine wiles on him for family advancement."

His laugh was brief, rather pointed. "Not to be unkind, Karen, you haven't got any. You're as alarmingly direct as a child!"

She bit on her underlip. "Subtle as a landslide, that's me!" Her eyes sparkled ironically. "I might surprise you by the time the night's over."

"I've not the slightest doubt about that. Now let me have a look at you." He turned her about to face him.

"I have a little of everything," she rattled on absurdly. "Two eyes, a nose . . ."

"You'll need a little more than that," he murmured imperturbably. "Eye-make up, perhaps. Trish will know all about that."

"You do yourself an injustice. I thought you were doing extremely well as a ladies' maid. In any case I don't bother much with all that junk."

"It's about time you did," he retorted bluntly.

Karen swirled half way across the room away from him, rather enjoying the lovely movement of her skirt. "An unnecessary gilding of the lily, I was brought up to believe." Her eyes touched on his dark face. "If you're trying to crush me, and

74

you are, I might tell you, you'll never succeed. I have inner resources."

There was a glimmer of something, not appraisal now, but approval in the depths of his eyes.

"And you'll need them if you consider I'm simply indulging you at the moment."

She smiled at him, her voice adding meaning to her words.

"You're always surprising me, Guy Amber. Some might be forgiven for thinking your actions extraordinarily high-handed."

His eyes gleamed. "I'm on the verge of pointing out ..." He broke off abruptly, turning towards the door. There was another light tap and Patricia Amber called softly:

"May I come in, please, Karen?"

Guy Amber laughed and walked to the door, opening it to admit his sister.

"Like an angel you always turn up when you're needed."

"And who needs me?" Dark laughing eyes came to rest on Karen's slender figure, only to widen slightly. "Why, Karen, you look like my Queen of Sheba!"

Karen smiled at this not too unexpected simile. The Queen of Sheba was one of Aunt Patricia's favourite orchids. She gave Guy a gleaming, sidelong look. "Due entirely to your brother's exquisite taste, Aunt Patricia."

He ignored her, a mannerism that was fast becoming a habit.

"I think she could do with a little more make-up for the evening, Trish. I'll leave it to you." He bent his dark head and brushed his sister's cheek. "You look very elegant, as usual, my dear."

"The eye of the beholder, perhaps, Guy."

Karen's eyes rested thoughtfully on the tall, graceful figure in glowing brocade. "But I think so too, Aunt Patricia," she burst out impulsively. "The years have touched you with the gentlest of fingers. You're as lovely now as I ever remembered you."

There was the tiniest of silences while the tears stood momentarily in the older woman's eyes. Karen's young voice faltered, ever sensitive to what went on about her. "I haven't upset you, have I?"

"Of course not!" Patricia Amber blinked rapidly. "Of course not, my dear," she repeated. "It's just sometimes . . . some trick . . ." She broke off, her eyes filled with a strange stillness.

"Well now, what about this make-up?" Guy came to stand beside his sister, lifting his eyebrows at her.

"Yes, of course! Karen won't know herself with a touch here and there." Patricia turned to her gaily, though her mouth trembled. "Your eyes are such a fabulous colour you'd do well to enhance their natural beauty." She took hold of her brother's arm and drew him to the door. "I'll be back in a moment. Karen. I have the very jewellery to pick up your gown."

After they were gone Karen stood silently for a moment, then walked to the mirror, addressing her reflection.

"So one way or the other, my poor foolish girl, you're going to the party looking *exactly* as Guy had intended!"

Philip at least was impressed. He was sitting up in his bed watching a very noisy programme on a portable T.V. Karen opened his door without knocking and came to stand at the foot of the bed. Philip looked up matter-of-factly, then did a double-take. Karen watched him switch off the set, smiling her astonishment.

"Good gracious, I would never have given you credit for that! Where did you get it from, anyway?" She inclined her head towards the set.

"From Aunt Trish," he said carelessly. "Honestly, Karo, you don't look a bit like yourself. Like Cinderella in those oven ads."

"Gosh, you'll have to do a bit better than that." Karen walked over to the dressing table and had another look at herself. Cinderella in the oven ads!

"No, really, Karo. You look terrific!" Philip began to bounce up and down in excessive admiration. "I can't explain." He continued to gaze at her while his mind made a long, painful detour. "I can't really see why you're going, and I'm not!"

Karen spun around, looking shocked. "Good grief, you ought to! There's quite a bit of difference between ten and nineteen, you know."

"I *do* know." Philip narrowed his eyes knowingly. "That makes me a slip-up."

Karen wheeled and came over to him, peering at him in astonishment. "I beg your pardon?"

Philip held her eyes, colouring slightly. "I said I guess I'm a slip-up. One of the kids in the class told me. When your brother or sister is years and years older than you, that makes you a slip-up."

Karen was torn between amusement and the necessity to correct him. "Let me tell you, Pip," she announced dryly, "you were no slip-up, whatever that might be. You always got the lion's share of Mother's attention, and Father, I remember, adored you. Besides, I don't think I care for that kind of talk."

Philip was contrite. "Sorry, Karo. I knew Murph didn't know what he was talking about. Always trying to be a smart alec."

"I suppose so," Karen smiled with sweet reasonableness. "Now don't have that thing going too long, Pip."

"Ah, come on, Karo. Just this once, seeing you're going to the party."

"Not at all, Pip." Karen's voice became firm. "Nine o'clock at the latest, and only because it's Saturday night." She bent and kissed his cheek. "Nine o'clock?" She looked into his face searchingly, exacting a promise.

"Nine o'clock!" Pip repeated, his eyes serene. "Besides, Aunt Trish is coming to collect it then. She doesn't trust me either."

Karen returned his grin and went to the door. "I'll tell you all about it in the morning."

"I bet you steal the show!" Pip called after her, then settled back on the pillows, turning on the set. Stealthily, he withdrew a half-eaten bar of chocolate from under one pillow, turning back the silver paper. Karo would kill him for going to bed without cleaning his teeth!

CHAPTER V

BELLE AMBER was a glitter of lights and cars were parked six deep on the drive. The great panelled doors between the living and the drawing rooms were thrown open dramatising the full fifty-foot scale of the central wing and displaying to dazzling advantage the pair of eighteenth-century Waterford chandeliers that hung from the moulded plaster ceilings.

The beautiful old house had been decorated in the most flexible of styles, allowing it to serve all the functions and moods of a family famous for their entertaining. To this end, all alterations and modifications to the original building had been carried out without sacrificing beauty, elegance or continuity of period. The large glass areas that opened up the back of the house admitted sunlight by day and afforded floodlit views of the pool and garden by night.

Karen came quickly down the stairway, stopping for a brief sideways glance in the gilded trumeau that hung above an antique cabinet in the hallway. Her reflection induced a gentle tingling in her veins such as a good wine might evoke. She could hold her own anywhere in this gown! From the great rooms came the mingled sound of laughter, excited voices and the music of an excellent trio. There was to be dancing on the terrace, food and wine on the patio. The house was filled with flowers and the scent of them reached her in soft fragrant drifts. Karen hesitated outside the living room, experiencing the uncertainty everyone does before being launched on a roomful of strangers. Within seconds, Patricia Amber was at her side.

"Karen darling! There are so many people I want you to meet." Her hand dropped lightly on Karen's arm. "And believe me, dear, you'd brighten up any party!" The little dimple flicked

79

beside her mouth. "Guy is on duty out on the terrace. He's fathoms deep in conversation with a very merry widow who's reputed to be on the look-out for a third husband. I do believe he wants you to play for us later on. Of course, if you don't want to, dear, you don't have to. I remember Stephen . . . your father . . . used to get tied up in knots before performing."

Karen smiled. "You never get over being nervous, Aunt Patricia, but I'd be happy to play for you whenever you like."

"Thank you, darling. Uncle Mark has never stopped singing your praises, so I don't really think you'd be able to get out of it even if you wanted to. Now, here's our first lot . . ." She leaned towards Karen conspiratorially. "They say parties are to women what battlefields are to men . . . so here goes!"

Karen laughed and allowed herself to become the centre of a bright ever-changing circle, full of vaguely familiar faces. They would be the Beautiful People, she supposed with an inward quirk of amusement. She smiled, she spoke, she answered, poised and lovely, all the time anxious to please Aunt Patricia, to have her feel proud of her. It was only when the circle thinned out a little that Rikki came to claim her. He looked very "with-it" and a far cry from the paint-spattered boy genius.

"Karo love, you look positively flamelike amongst all this weak candle power! I swear I've got that queer feeling you get when exposed to real beauty." Suddenly laughing, he whirled her out on to the terrace, the chiffon of her skirt swirling in liquid brightness. "Well, have you met all these perfectly wonderful people?"

"Just about!" Karen looked up at him, her eyes slightly bewitched with excitement. He gave her his rare, reckless grin.

"You've got to marry me, Karo, sooner or later. I've been giving it some thought and it seems like the very best solution. We'll head off to somewhere far-flung and I'll paint you in every possible guise." He slid his arms around her waist and started out on the downbeat of the dance tune. "You should really be grateful. I come into a small fortune when I'm twenty-five."

He swung her out on to the floor, smiling at her serene indifference to his expected wealth.

"You've been drinking!" she observed matter-of-factly.

"Of course I've been drinking. I mistrust anyone who doesn't at parties." Other couples surged round them and he drew further down the length of the terrace. She relaxed in his arms with a swift, upward smile. "I like you, Rikki. I always have and I guess I always will."

"I knew I could make you respond to my cherubic charm."

Karen broke into a laugh. "You might *look* cherubic, but I happen to know you've a mercurial temperament. Don't forget I grew up with you."

"I know nothing of the kind — we've just met!" His light, teasing voice dropped a full octave. "Now there's a real Scott Fitzgerald heroine for you. She dances on tables and drinks gallons of gin."

Karen followed his gaze and saw a delectable slightly overweight redhead in coffee cream lace.

"Sue Paton, the heiress?"

"The same one. She's been after Guy for the best part of her girlhood and she's now thirty-five. Doesn't look it, does she? Guy can't very well avoid her, they move in the same circles, but he always lines up a counter-attraction for her at parties. That's him, the rather debauched-looking character sitting on a few millions. Never leaves anything to chance, our Guy!"

The music stopped and pairs broke up and merged into laughing groups. A waiter came through the French doors with a tray of champagne, then the music, muted and dreamy, throbbed through the house again and Rikki drew her back into his arms.

Karen, looking over his shoulder, caught sight of Liane in a blue, very feminine extravaganza, threading her way across the terrace towards them.

"Here's Liane. She looks faintly upset about something." Rikki groaned and gave up. "This is not the time to say it, but couldn't you have checked out Liane's outfit? That's pure Hollywood, and the forties at that."

"Please don't say anything to that effect, Rikki. You wouldn't want to destroy her confidence!"

Rikki gritted his teeth.

"That's being well taken care of! Poor old Lee. She's just a satellite." His blue eyes looked unhappy and slightly cynical. "A satellite in orbit around mother moon."

Karen laid a warning hand on his arm. Liane reached them, her dark eyes wide and anxious.

"Mother's been detained. That was Colin on the phone, now. It will take them the best part of an hour to get here."

"That's the most wonderful news in the whole wide world," Rikki said brightly.

"Everything's all right, isn't it?" Karen cut in, over the top of Rikki.

"Yes, of course." Liane looked from one to the other. "I'm just a bit anxious. Colin drives so very fast when he's late for an appointment."

"Don't worry, he has such precious cargo," Rikki pointed out unfeelingly. "By the way, sweetie, you don't need all those frill and furbelows around your neck, do you? I like you uncluttered, like Trish. You've got the same line."

Liane looked down at her foaming neckline. "Don't you like it?"

"Not much. You'd have plenty of time to change. What about that coral affair Trish bought you?"

"Oh, don't be silly, Rikki, it's much too plain for tonight." Liane dismissed the idea. "Colin will love this. It's Celia's choice, after all, and you have to admit she has perfect taste."

"A positive flair for perfection, if you ask me," Rikki drawled lightly. "But for *herself*, kiddo. You've got to study your own type. Celia can't do it for you."

"Oh, don't start that again, Rikki." Liane looked to Karen for approval.

"I'm sure Colin will think you look lovely," Karen managed, even if she agreed wholeheartedly with Rikki. One couldn't very well start picking Liane to pieces. It would be extremely hurtful and quite the wrong time and wrong place for it.

"Rikki!" A tall, horsey young woman with nut-brown hair and brown eyes and a very assured manner advanced on them, putting her arm through Rikki's. "I've some perfectly wonderful friends of mine dying to meet you." She flickered a glance and a "You'll excuse us!" at the two younger girls and drew an unenthusiastic Rikki through the maze of guests.

Liane expelled her long-held breath. "You've got to hand it to Rikki, he's never anyone else but himself. It's quite funny the way he can't understand he's terribly eligible, though Roz Mazlin would chase him if he had buck teeth and a squint. She makes no secret of her plans for marrying money. Bucket-loads of it, I understand." Her white teeth glinted behind her full coral mouth. "I won't be a moment, Karo. I'd better tell Aunt Trish about Mother and Colin. I do hope they make it before supper." She looked at Karen with mock solemnity. "You'll have to watch yourself tonight, Karo. I've heard some pretty extravagant comments. You look like being the newest sensation."

"If she is, then I'm here to look after her!"

Liane swung around, amused. "I'm sort of interested in hearing what *you* think, Guy, as a connoisseur of beautiful women."

"I feel we need a little more time," he drawled, his dark eyes on Karen.

Liane's answering nod was dead serious. Her eyes veered to Karen. "I know you're going to like Colin. I'll introduce you just as soon as he arrives."

Guy watched her retreating figure. "Many waters cannot quench love, neither can floods drown it. Colin seems to have fallen on his feet, and Lee's much too young for such things."

"And you're a judge of love?" Karen arched her slender

83

neck to gaze away from him into the garden, pierced with shafts of rose and gold.

"Now why sound so scornful?" He gave a brief laugh. "Come dance with me."

"I might bungle it," she said lightly.

His dark eyes were amused. "I don't mind. Tonight I'm all loving kindness, even towards a spitting kitten. I've done my duty towards all the dull, really important people, and now I have you."

"I'm speechless!" She pretended abstraction and looked over his shoulder at the whirling vortex of couples.

"Come here!"

She went into his arms, feeling them close round her, hearing his voice but not hearing it. This curious effect he had on her, there must be some chemical explanation for it, but sensation was making logic remote.

"Decorative *and* silent, as a young girl should be!" His voice had an unmistakable thread of laughter in it.

"I can see I'll have to do better. Splendid night, isn't it?" She looked up at him, then suddenly mindful of something, began to flutter her eyelashes, riveting his attention.

"What on earth is that all about?" he asked, his eyes narrowing. "You look quite absurd."

"Fancy! And your own idea after all! I'm merely giving you the benefit of my dramatic eye make-up." She trailed off under his sardonic look, and a hint of admiration came into his eyes.

"Not bad! Not bad at all!" he laughed softly, and drew her closer, Karen willed her limbs not to tremble. With a little maturity she could handle this situation, but his dark arrogance simply shrivelled her bones even if her head remained perfectly clear. Unconsciously she moved near him like a magnet drawn on an irresistible path.

"You're trembling, Karen," he observed conversationally.

"Just a mild form of hysteria," she answered very dryly. "I'm sure you're used to it."

A flame licked up in his dark eyes. "I would have thought you were immune. In fact, you've been very vocal about it."

She couldn't suppress the mischief in her eyes. "Perhaps I've a very realistic approach to life."

"Now don't women say idiot things!" He met her wide, jewel-bright eyes. "There's no need to look at me with so much concentrated inquiry."

"That would seem to be a woman's vocation," she murmured laconically.

There was an undercurrent of mockery in the depths of his eyes. "Now I would have thought that was to be loved!"

She pushed back against his arm. "This is a pleasantly meaningless conversation, isn't it?"

"Could it be otherwise with a babe in the woods?"

"Well, you'd certainly qualify for one of the other leading parts!"

He looked at her through half-closed lids. "Now don't spare me, Karen. I can face up to my limitations."

Her voice was silky. "Surely you're not waiting for me to agree with that? By the way, there's a mermaid swimming against the drapes with a long straight fall of blonde hair who's making me feel very guilty and uncomfortable at the moment."

"Miaow!" he smiled very slightly. "She's very good at it — the competitive type. Name the game and she'll beat you at it."

"Well, you may be used to this kind of thing, but I can't bear to be the target of so much distilled suspicion."

Guy hazed his cheek over her dark hair, adding insult to injury, and Karen drew away from him very pointedly.

"I don't think I care to be used as a *muleta* — the red flag, you know."

"I did guess at its meaning," he drawled lazily. "I've spent a little time in Spain."

She sighed briefly and relaxed in his arms.

"When this dance is over I shall be a woman of experience."

"I prefer you as you are!"

Her eyes met his, half laughing, half provocative. "And how is that?"

"Oh, rather magical and mysterious."

Her breath caught suddenly. "Don't do it to me, Guy," she said huskily. "For all you know I might be an idiot child."

"Only in as much as you like your own way."

"I'm only human, I admit, while you, of course, are a machine, and no woman is going to gum up the machinery."

"How clever of you, my exclusive beauty."

"If I'm boring you, please stop," she said in a voice not her own.

"You may annoy me, but never bore me, I imagine."

Karen hoped she didn't look as keyed up as she felt. His hold tightened on her.

"Now, now, take it easy. Your eyes are shimmering with the most feverish intensity. I told you before, I'd never hurt you."

"If only I could believe that!" she announced rather oddly in the long stillness, then yielded completely to his encircling arm.

Shortly before supper, Patricia Amber went in search of Karen, and found her in the drawing room, being lectured on the architectural quality of its detailed Corinthian columns and handsome wall panelling. Her tutor was a fair, short-sighted, very serious young man called Jeffrey Parrish, whose father held the Chair of Architecture at the University. His father, an attractive widower, also at the party, was exhibiting his aesthetic tastes by spending the best part of the evening on the love seat with Gina Holmes, the well-known fashion-model.

Karen's amused eyes flickered backwards and forwards between father and son, giving the son only half her attention. Her delight in her surroundings, Jeffrey was telling her, was not only instinctive but drawn largely from unconscious experience. Appreciation, he explained was the critical weighing of all qualities, good and bad, while taste, and Jeffrey bowed to her, was the preference for the good qualities and the conscious choice of them.

Karen tried to look suitably impressed.

"I think we could safely say the one and only test of appreciation is delight!" Jeffrey said emphatically. Karen, her eyes on the love seat, had to agree.

"That statement must, of course, be qualified." The young man spun quickly, prevented from elaborating by his hostess's detaining arm on his sleeve.

"I wonder if I might borrow Karen for a moment, please, Jeffrey. She's going to play for us!"

"The *piano*?" Jeffrey's fair eyebrows disappeared under his hair. "I say, I've never actually spoken to a girl who could *play* the piano. They've had lessons, of course, but they can't actually *play*." He trailed in their wake, one hand on his lapel, with the deference Karen felt should possibly be accorded to Royalty.

The room quietened with disconcerting suddenness as Aunt Patricia announced her and Karen went to the piano, conscious of Mark Amber's encouraging nod and the quick assessing glance of the trio's pianist. Guy opened up the lid of the Steinway as Karen reached it and she swallowed rather nervously.

His eyes were intent. "You're nervous! You've lost colour!"

"Of course I'm nervous," she said barely above a whisper.

"You wouldn't be worth a bumper if you weren't!" His eyes held hers for a moment, his presence a good sedative, even an antidote for her present mood of pre-performance nerves.

"Play your usual *tour de force*," he suggested. "There's no sense in letting them all go to sleep on us."

Karen settled herself on the piano seat, pitching her voice for him alone.

"You're taking an awful risk, aren't you? I could be the merest amateur. Think of your friends!"

"Right now I'm thinking of you, and I know all about the Conservatorium diploma!"

His dark eyes swept her face, supremely confident, whether of her or himself or both of them Karen had no means of telling. She gave him an entirely false, sweet smile. "Thank you, Guy!"

"Thank *you*, little one." He moved away from the piano and she was on her own, with the room expectantly quiet about her.

A *tour de force*, Guy said. Well, there was always Chopin's famous study, the so-called Revolutionary Etude. It was filled with innumerable technical difficulties but cloaked for the listener with the beauty and emotion of a spontaneous work of art.

With the opening chord, Karen settled and the music surged into the room, proud, rebellious and full of passionate nationalism. Her left hand was impeccable as it had to be, its movements broad and sweeping from long hours of practice. Her first choice was but a prelude to her second. The audience, hard core sophisticates for the most part, were entirely charmed. It was something of a novelty for a beautiful girl to be so gifted and *so* unexpected!

There was the merest break to establish the mood, then Karen went straight into her "party piece" from Conservatorium days – Liszt's Mephisto Waltz. It poured out like a torrent, as did the unqualified applause. She bowed her slender white nape in acknowledgment, conscious of having given of her best. Mark Amber ensconced in a bergère in the corner, surrounded by his own particular friends, tilted his glass to her. She smiled in his direction and took Guy's outstretched hand. Her own hands were trembling now with a sudden draining of nervous energy. His hand tightened, the thumb caressing her palm, easing the tension out of her. He had far too many tricks to him!

"For a special occasion, there's always a special treat! I have something lined up for you, little one. Are you interested?"

"Frankly I'm intrigued!" She turned away to smile into faces that smiled back at her with heightened interest.

"You play beautifully, Karen," he added gravely.

"We learn something new every day." Excitement made her flippant. His dark eyes rested on her ivory face, the colour now returning to it.

"I said you *play* beautifully, little one, but in many respects your education has been sadly neglected."

"I'm sure you'll see to it," she returned sweetly.

"But are you sure you can stick the course?"

She smiled without answering, not even knowing how to answer him.

"Where are you taking me?"

"How far would you be prepared to go, I wonder?" His manner seemed to convey some secret challenge.

"Not very far with you, Guy Amber!"

He tut-tutted gently. "That's hardly fair and very misguided. You're palpitating like a bird under my hand. Does it affect you so very much, then?"

Her eyes, wide and startled, flew to his.

"Playing the piano," he stressed dryly.

"Of course!" She looked away from him hastily, following blindly until they came to the door of the private cellar. Guy pulled the heavy door and switched on a light. It flashed its beam over a steep flight of stone steps.

"I'll go first. Keep straight behind me and go carefully in that long skirt."

Karen narrowed her eyes against the naked bulb, seeing high walls lined with solidly constructed wine racks, stacked with meticulous care. The necks of the bottles, capped with coloured aluminium or lead alloy foil, protruded from the racks, turned on their sides to keep the corks moist and prevent them from shrinking.

There were table wines, red and white, sparkling wines, champagne, the oak casks of fortified wines, the sherries, the brandies, the port and dessert wines, the spirits and liqueurs. Each bin was dated and each bottle entered and catalogued in the cellar book.

Her attention distracted, Karen's foot, in its light evening shoe, missed the third step. Her heart lurched with the sickening realisation that she was falling.

"Guy!" she cried out like a wounded bird.

He turned swiftly, his senses alerted before actual danger. His broad shoulders braced themselves against the single rail as he took her full weight, cradling her against him and smothering her face and hair against the beautiful blackcloth of his evening jacket. They stood there motionless, for a minute, while her heart flipped, then righted itself.

She lifted her face to him, her hair spilling back over her shoulders.

"Oh, I'm sorry, Guy. I would have fallen. You did warn me. It was my sandal – the sole is so new and shiny." Her perfume seemed to be in the air, on both of them, spiking the cool atmosphere, elusive yet persistent.

He laughed in his throat. "Excuses, excuses – and you're such a devil of a weight! Well, this should take care of the sandals." He swung her up into his arms, her flame-coloured gown foaming about her. A sensation akin to sharpest, not-to-be-borne excitement took hold of her.

"Now what are you afraid of?" he taunted her. "You can't come to that much harm!"

At the base of the stairs he held her for a moment longer, looking down into her face. "To hear you play one would never think there was so little of you."

The expression in her topaz eyes changed elusively. "Don't you like thin girls?"

His dark eyes were amused, raking her mercilessly. "I wouldn't have said you were *thin*, precisely."

"In that case, you'd better put me down." She looked back at him rather helplessly.

Guy laughed and lowered her gently to the floor, his back blocking the light.

"Mark tells me you've never tasted champagne."

"No!" she said, her attention diverted, "but there's plenty to be had upstairs."

He smiled. "Not quite the same. In any case, you haven't had any all evening."

She shot him a look of inquiry. "How do you know? You've been so . . . busy," she murmured dryly.

"Busy or not, I can always keep an eye on you."

Karen looked away from his mouth, speaking airily. "Actually I wouldn't be game to touch even a sherry before playing. It's disastrous, no matter what anyone else may tell you."

He laughed and moved over to the circular oak table that stood between the wine racks. At the back of the table was a cabinet, holding glasses, and on top of the cabinet an ice bucket. Only then did Karen notice the bottle reclining in it, with its elegant French label and *appellation d'origine contrôlée*.

Guy took it down and put it on the small table. "The unique quality of champagne is that it suits any occasion. I don't think you could say the same for any other wine. My grandmother used to drink it for breakfast, though she *was* a trifle eccentric. Some of our own champagnes are excellent, but they're not yet in the same class as the great French champagnes. I want you to try the best. Your palate is unsullied." He removed the wired-down cork, expertly controlling the natural effervescence of the wine.

Karen's eyes were sparkling. "This is quite exciting!"

"I thought you'd think so."

"A typical reaction, perhaps?" she smiled up at him, the mischief and significance apparent in her eyes.

"*Not* so typical!" His voice was very dry. "I can see quite plainly that your eyes are sparkling solely in anticipation of the wine." He took out two glasses, short-stemmed tulips, a perfect combination of size, shape and thinness, and near filled them. "Don't expect to get the best from the *wine* if you use the open-mouthed coupe for champagne, Karen, though you might get the best from the occasion. This is a mixture of three parts *pinot noir* to one part *pinot blanc*, a blend by the bottle fermentation method, of course. All good champagnes are bottle fermented, as you know." He held up the glass to the light, and the liquid scintillated the colour of pale straw. "I suppose you know if the black grapes are allowed to become too ripe it's impossible to avoid some colour in the wine, that's why the grapes must be picked at exactly the right time and handled very carefully before they reach the crushers. I'll take you over Amberleigh when we go interstate."

"I'll keep you to that," she said, her eyes brilliant over the rim of the glass.

"No need. That's a promise!" He held up his own glass. "To your beautiful eyes, little one!"

Karen buried her nose in the wineglass, trying to capture the elusive bouquet.

He laughed. "If you do *that*, my child, you're very likely to sneeze! The escaping carbon dioxide gets into the nose before the bouquet impinges."

Karen tried again, taking a mouthful and savouring the exquisitely dry flavour. He watched her, half smiling, as she finished the glass and handed it back to him.

"Nothing's ever tasted so ambrosial – the sum of perfection! I'll have another, please."

There was indulgence in the curve of his mouth. She smiled at him then, a child's smile, very sweet and innocent, devoid of the veneer of sophistication. The light threw a nimbus of gold around her head, shadowed hollows on her cheeks and a bloom over her skin.

"Karen, Karen," he said softly, "you look *exactly* as you used to look ... oh, ten or more years ago." A kind of amusement seemed to play in his eyes.

"And you're *exactly* as shattering as you ever were, Guy Amber!"

"You say that very emphatically, little one." He handed her glass back to her.

"Occasionally the reckless side of my nature gets the better of me." She gave a small helpless shrug of her shoulder, feeling she was being whirled into danger. "We'd better go back, hadn't we?" She sipped at her wine, waiting for an answer.

He looked back at her, faintly smiling. "There's plenty of time!" A dark glitter of magnetic current spun out between them. He drained his own glass and refilled it. Karen tried to fix her attention on negative things ... the dull sheen of the table, the multi-coloured tops of aluminium foil ... She moistened her top lip, tasting champagne.

"Relax, little one! You'd drive a man crazy!"

"I'd drive a man crazy!" She accented the first word strangely. Her voice sounded excited and just a little overwrought.

"Now it's your turn to be polite," he smiled at her lazily, black brows slanting.

An exhausted sweetness seemed to come over her.

"You're the very devil, Guy! I feel utterly breathless."

"And you look utterly charming and just a tiny bit irresponsible."

"It's the champagne! It seems to transcend ordinary spheres for a while." Her voice grew dreamy, reflective. "If I shut my eyes I can travel back in time to the beautiful days ... the fine, unforgettable days, so tangible I can feel the brush of the air, the smell of the earth, the flood of rising sunlight washing over the vineyards, the foothills ... Pip's pure profile, the baby texture of his skin ... my mother. Father, so gay and handsome ... Aunt Patricia ... *you*!" Her eyes flew open. His dark face was very near her, his eyes oddly brilliant. "You're dangerous!" The words seemed torn from her. She retreated a few steps, her eyes fixed on his face, almost spellbound, fighting the crazy urge to get into his arms.

"Yes, you're dangerous!" she repeated in a soft intense undertone. "I don't know what this is all about, but it's got to stop!" Her hand swept the air between them, forcibly expressive.

His laugh, brief and highly amused, eased the tension.

"The champagne has gone to your head, my pet. Whatever it is I want from you, you're not capable of giving it . . . at the moment." He smiled at her tilted profile. "Look at me, Karen. Finish your drink and we'll go upstairs. You're only a babe!"

"I'm very glad I am," she said simply. "You're rather frightening, Guy. You give me the distinct impression that women are only for evening, to be forgotten when the sun comes up and there's work to be done."

"You should be spanked for that!"

"By whom?"

"Me! Either way you're much too young to kiss."

She put her glass down carefully and swirled away from him, moving towards the steps. He caught her up easily, keeping a steadying hand at her waist.

"And then she fled me!" he murmured mockingly in her ear.

"Thank you for the *champagne*," she said quickly, holding up her long skirt, trying to beat him up the stairs.

His hand brushed her flushed cheek as he leaned forward to open the door for her.

"I'm glad you were able to appreciate it, little one. I haven't enjoyed myself so much in years!"

Rikki, coming through from the entrance hall, stalked up to them with a comic expression of outrage. "In a democracy there ought to be an equal distribution of privilege. Who's been sampling the best bubbly?"

Guy's mouth faintly quirked. "We have been indulging in that wicked extravagance, Rikki. But your vigil of waiting is over. You may take Karen in to supper."

Rikki peered intently into Karen's face. Her cheeks bore a faint almond blossom flush. "I was scared rotten that wouldn't be the case. A big wheeler-dealer like Guy usually rides roughshod over all the competition, puts them down with a word."

Guy's voice was mild. "Let's go in, Rick. Trish will be wanting to start supper." His reappearance signalled the start of the buffet supper: the lobster, the oysters, the prawn and avocado cocktails, the caviar with cucumber, the crab ramekins, the chicken and curries with piles of steaming snowy white rice, the tossed green salads with crusty French bread, the chocolate and chestnut cheesecakes, the brandied peaches, gingered apples, flaming strawberries, the little flagged cheeses of five different countries and a wonderful selection of wines.

The lights glowed on the vari-coloured dresses of the women, the suave black and white, the maroon, midnight blue and deep amethyst jackets of the men.

"Such beautiful harmonies!" Karen's voice in Rikki's ear was soft and rapturous. "The deep sensuous pleasure of fine china and silver, beautiful crystal and immaculate napery!" Her glance swept the table. "Not to mention the food!"

Rikki was giving it his full attention. The guests crowded into the tables and impulsively Karen drew closer to him, chattering and laughing, just the two of them, young and with each other, unguarded.

"You're thinking I'm just a little bit intoxicated, now aren't you?" Karen smiled into Rikki's intense, young face.

"I'm thinking how ... beautiful you are," he answered with complete candour. The throaty little laugh she gave was just as unselfconscious and charming as a child's.

"You improve by the minute!"

"Ditto!" Rikki smiled, and continued to pile up their plates; not even consulting Karen for her preferences. But it was delicious and Karen could feel herself begin to take wings.

"Your eyes are melting in that weird way again, Karo. It's a trick that's interfering very seriously with my breathing."

"Not your *eating*!" she pointed out dryly, watching him spear yet another prawn cutlet. "I hope you're not going to talk like a blithering idiot all evening?"

"Words to live by, Miss Hartmann. Blithering idiot, indeed!

I have news for you, dear girl. I'm not mad."

She laughed at him with affection. "I know."

Rikki's eyes gleamed a hectic and brilliant blue and she had a very clear picture of the enormous attraction a few extra years would bring him. "You're enchanting," he said softly. "For me, I hope?"

She sipped at her wine, her small elegant head slightly tipped to one side. "Do you want a frank answer? Not for anyone."

Rikki grinned, a wide, disarming grin. "Was that supposed to be a squelch?"

"What a ridiculous and spiteful suggestion! In actual fact, I'm still dreaming of the perfect admirer."

His tone and look shrivelled her. "The perfect admirer – and with me around! 'I am half sick of shadows, cried the Lady of Shalott?' "

Karen laughed. "Do you often quote Tennyson?"

"Only when I drift into the doldrums. I thought you were well on the way to loving me."

"I can't help what you think." She looked away from him to smile across the table at Mark Amber, who waggled his wineglass at her. Rikki was unabashed.

"I suppose love is a bit dicey, at that. A state of mind more than anything else. Take all the great lovers ... Beatrice and Dante, Romeo and Juliet, Tristan and Isolde, Fred and Maggie. You couldn't really say they knew one another. Strangers, you might say. I can't really see that great love and day-to-day living go hand in hand."

Karen almost choked and Rikki patted her kindly.

"I can see you've grasped the realities of the situation," she managed at last.

"I wish to God I had!"

Karen looked puzzled into his face. For the first time Rikki's voice was devoid of humour.

"All this and modesty too?" she asked lightly.

His expression changed. "I suppose you know what you're saying, Karo. You're practically admitting you're feeling the pull of my fascination."

"My mind is on higher things," she pointed out, her eyes roaming over the room.

"That's what I'm afraid of," Rikki muttered *sotto voce*, noting without surprise the direction in which her eyes were constantly straying. Suddenly he glanced over his shoulder. "Do you hear?" He put his wineglass on the table, his face inscrutable. From somewhere behind them came a voice; a voice Karen was to come to know far too well. It was a soft, sweet voice with a faint trace of husky allure. Instinctively she straightened, aware of a sudden, unaccountable tension. She tried to relax again, but she was too sensitive to Rikki's mental and physical attitude, at once alert and wary.

Then she was there! Celia Amber — framed in the doorway, poised with the studied grace that irresistibly recalled to Karen's mind the entrance of a great actress, awaiting the applause which was her due. With such a face and figure and acting ability, Karen thought inconsequentially, it was a wonder Hollywood hadn't beaten a path to her door. One moment only and she had the lasting impression of exquisite slenderness, of vivid blue eyes and an aureole of silver-gilt hair.

"Guy!" the soft husky voice sang the name, for him alone. "Darling," she stretched out her hands to him, breathless, "I've been frantic ... simply *frantic*! It's just been one of those end-of-the-world days! Trish!" She gazed wide-eyed at her much taller sister-in-law, as she separated herself from her guests. A well-dressed, smooth-faced young man hovered on the periphery of the group. Colin! Karen thought with instant dismay, not quite sure why she was so disappointed.

"Stone the crows!" Rikki murmured succinctly. "The kittenish girl-child!"

Karen looked at him quickly, all the time hearing the soft husky voice, the breathless little pauses that punctuated the bursts of explanations. Heads were lifting and greetings called and exchanged. Celia smiled and waved with charm and animation, so obviously home again, among her own admiring crowd. She circled the room like a swan, tiptoed to brush her daughter's cheek, then she was coming towards them.

Rikki went rigid. "Rikki dearest!" One white arm stole through her son's, whose shoulder she barely reached. Then the blue eyes were on Karen with extraordinary vividness. There was no liking there, no warmth, nor even dislike; just a hard clear assessment like a bolt of merchandise she found vaguely unbelievable.

The expression broke so quickly Karen very nearly convinced herself she had imagined it. The voice was warm, still sweet, yet to Karen's over-sensitive ears, gently accusing.

"Why . . . why, Karen, you're quite *pretty*. I never dreamed . . . you used to be such a *fey* little thing, all long legs and big eyes!"

"Lord love me!" Rikki's snort heralded an attack. "Isn't that the understatement of the year. *Pretty!* Karen's quite beautiful!"

"Do you hear him?" The blue eyes looked from Karen, who prickled uncomfortably to her son. "Beautiful, he says!" Despite the cool, elegant little laugh that went with it Karen knew quite plainly that Celia wasn't amused. A slight tartness entered her sweet voice. "You get more like the Ambers every day, my darling, but you do have a certain indestructible quality."

"To the hills!" said Rikki, but Celia ignored him. She turned her attention to Karen. "I'm so sorry I wasn't able to meet you earlier, Karen. You do understand." Her tiny fine-boned hand lifted with a gesture of complete helplessness. "That Colin! He's such a capable young man when he's himself, but really . . ." her voice trilled with laughter and her eyes gleamed with something like triumph . . . "he's not himself!"

Karen was staring unashamedly. So this was Aunt Celia?

Rikkie and Liane's mother? Uncle Mark was quite right, she would never have recognised her again. The silver-gilt hair — it had never been that colour, although it was Rikki's exactly — was fluffed high on the crown with a fringe of soft bangs that melted into the pearly tones of her brow. Her eyelids were moulded closely over her deeply blue eyes, her nose short, slightly tilted, the lower lip full, the upper a trifle short, the skin without blemish, the contours of the face smoother, more clear-cut than ever before. Her evening gown of chiffon and white lace was perfection, cut low in the bodice, her figure as firm and youthful as a young girl's. Celia Amber was incredible. She looked only a handful of years older than her son.

Karen tried to smile naturally. Her mouth moved and the muscles of her face went about their appointed business. She found herself replying, saying that it didn't matter in the least ... not to worry ... how wonderful it was to see her ... the family ...

The luminous smile persisted. Celia listened, her proud little head slightly tilted to the taller Karen. Her quickened breath moved the fragile lace at her breast. She spun her head with sweet imperativeness. "Come back, darling! Do excuse me, children. Have fun." She swirled away from them in a sea of chiffon, a lingering trace of expensive perfume.

It was impossible to mistake who *darling* was. Guy Amber, his arm thrust casually through a friend's, lifted his dark head with its definable grace of sculpture. Deep inside of her Karen screamed a passionate protest. Darling! An unreasonable revulsion began to oppress her like a heavy cloak.

Guy was smiling, giving his sister-in-law a charming, slightly formal bow.

"Honestly, darling, someone up there actually arranges these setbacks for me when I'm going out!" Celia's voice floated back to the table. Karen watched Guy move his hand in a gesture that made all explanations unimportant. He looked so tall, so sophisticated, so successful and worldly, with the arrogant simplicity of his beautiful, expensive clothes, she felt slightly ill just looking at him. Why should he have this damnable effect on her? Rikki, in his own way, was almost as eye-catching.

Celia, superb in her self-confidence, raised her white arms to Guy and then they were dancing. Celia was an exquisite carnation he wore on his jacket — impossible to believe they were not perfectly matched! Karen sighed deeply, her appetite and high spirits — gone. Around her heart she felt the clutch of something like raw jealously, but she still had enough common sense to dispatch it quickly. She glanced onced more at Rikki, only to find him just as desolate.

"Purely out of regard for my feelings, don't say anything," he warned her.

"I don't know what you're talking about!"

"I think you do, my pet. You've very quick and delicate perceptions. Besides, it's not the first time I've seen that particular calamity. If there was to be a new heaven and a new earth, Celia would have Guy on both of them. Come to that, do you suppose there's a woman here who wouldn't be mad to have Guy make love to her? He, of course, with that wonderful arrogant habit of his, never gives a damn! He's really got more sex appeal than is actually decent." Rikki's young voice held a measure of envy.

"Leave me out of it," Karen said with fiery disdain.

Rikki looked deeply into her flashing eyes. "Your type is rapidly becoming obsolete, my girl." He glanced over her shoulder and gave an audible groan. "Look out, here comes the fiancé, all goggle-eyed. On to a free meal ticket for life, he is. Still the thickets are full of wolves!"

Colin came up and was promptly introduced. At closer quarters he was still a disappointment, though with his thick brown hair, smooth tanned skin and large hazel eyes, he had more than the usual quota of good looks. His manner towards Rikki was faintly patronizing.

"Evening, Rick. When are you going to join up with us?

P.R. could do with a good man."

Rikki's expression was hard to beat. **"You've** been out in the midday sun," he said calmly, and glanced across at Karen. "If you'll excuse me for a moment, Karo, I'll just go and twist the tiger's tail."

"What an extremely odd young man!" Colin announced in a tone of shocked righteousness, watching Rikki make a bee-line towards his mother.

"Do you think so?"

Colin redirected his hazel gaze. "Well, he does seem to deal in half phrases and innuendoes. I'm never sure whether he's actually saying something to me or not."

Karen laughed and Colin perked up. He asked her to dance, holding her too firmly, and Karen's spirits plunged.

"I say, what do you think of Celia? She's fab, isn't she? Absolutely gorgeous. I don't see anyone to match her for looks and style. And her clothes – she wears them like nothing in this world. I ask you!"

Karen hoped her smile wasn't too tight. "Well then, I'll just have to say I've taken a strong and immediate liking to her."

Colin gave a small, hooting laugh. "What more could you want! Strange, that. Celia usually has all the girls pea green, but then you're rather fab yourself, aren't you?" He bent his head for a closer examination. "Yes, you are," he reiterated slowly. Karen closed her eyes. Her partner took this as an admission of pure enjoyment and drew her yet closer, his breath stirring her hair. He began to tell her of the many and spectacular business assignments to his credit, mistaking her limpid indifference for genuine admiration. On his own admission Colin was an excellent diagnostician with a natural flair for putting his finger on trouble.

Karen opened her eyes briefly. "How very alarming!" Conversation, however one-sided, ground to a halt.

Colin was flustered, afraid he might have given the wrong impression. "I think Guy himself would be the first to admit

I'm an asset to the firm." His expression contracted into peevishness.

Karen was prepared to admit that that might be the case, but she very much doubted Colin's ability to make Liane happy. Colin appeared to be a self-confessed egoist. She flashed Rikki a set of distress signals and he came immediately to her rescue. Liane was swept once more into her fiancé's arms, where she clearly longed to be.

"Back to the play-pen," Rikki murmured into Karen's ear.

All through the rest of the evening, Karen fought to keep her eyes off Celia and Guy. Guy seemed to be playing the gallant to Celia's charm with an urbanity Karen had hitherto never encountered. Yet why should she have hit on the word "playing" unless it was Guy's manner, so sardonic, so mocking, so blatant, it must surely be suspect unless it was real!

A tumult surged through her veins, the cause of which she was loath to put a name to. Instead she fell back on her old line of defence, inwardly blaming Guy for creating intolerable situations. Once more he was the villain of a melodrama.

The party, however, was a stunning success. Karen, had she known it, was proving quite a talking point. Malicious and witty tongues found occasion to remark on her youth and distinctive beauty and its possible repercussions in such a household. Her resemblance to her dead father was commented on and the old stories began to recirculate. One thing was certain, Celia Amber now had a powerful rival in the sphere of sheer glamour and one she was unlikely to tolerate. Horror of horrors, said the wits, the rival was young! – the unforgivable crime.

Long after the last guests had departed Karen was still wandering aimlessly about her room, unable to bring herself to the serious business of undressing. She felt over excited, off balance and curiously frustrated. At least she had played well, and some part of her took pleasure in the many sincere compliments that came her way with the farewells. She glanced down at her hands, noticing for the first time that she was not wearing the beautiful topaz dress ring Aunt Trish had lent her. Of course she had left it on the piano. She never could bear a ring on her finger when she played. She only hoped it would still be there. How forgetful and careless!

With sudden impatience she flew out of the room, down the long corridor, towards the staircase. The house was quite deserted now, with only a few lights on. There was not even an echo of the music, the laughter, that had resounded through the house only a few short hours before.

She came on down the stairs on whispering feet, her hand going to her heart as a dark velvet voice startled her.

"I might have known you'd be walking abroad like a witch after midnight!" Guy came round the base of the stairwell, looking up at her mockingly. "Perhaps you've come to tell me what you haven't told me all night. Did you like your party?"

Karen stood silently, trying to penetrate the façade of his easy, urban manner.

"Well, little Miss-in-her-teens?" His face was too smooth to be readable, but his voice was definitely sardonic.

"*My* party!" she said, looking at him strangely, but not making any movement towards him.

"I never know what you're getting at when you look at me like that. Tell me what's on your mind, child."

The light from a wall bracket enfolded and caressed her; her face and her shoulders, the slender line to her body. She stood for a moment almost defiantly, her head high and challenging.

"I can't see myself adopting so drastic a measure. At least, not with *you*!"

Dark laughter sprang into his eyes. There was a wholly appraising, masculine look on his handsome face.

"Could you be back to your imaginative fancies, I wonder?" he asked softly, his eyes narrowing.

She gave a bitter-sweet little laugh. "How astute you are, Guy, and so very sure of yourself. But I imagine keeping your emotions under control is elementary training for a business tycoon."

He took a step nearer her. "What a one you are for words! Sly as a kitten's paw. Don't tell me you've overheard some story put about by unfriendly elements?"

"I was brought up in a good home, so I can't tell you," she said, carried away on a tide of sheer recklessness.

"You've no sense of self-preservation, have you, my love?"

At once she sensed the change in him and knew a peculiar joy in arousing his temper.

"And now I don't know what *you* mean," she said sweetly, "though I couldn't help noticing the interest you took in all the good-looking women at the party."

"In only *one* woman, actually, but you wouldn't know anything about that." Their voices were clashing now, like weapons in the soft quietness.

Her eyes flashed in uncontrollable resentment. One woman! "Personally I think that sort of thing can be overdone. People can put two and two together!"

"And it still doesn't make five!" He moved then, slashing and ruthless, jerking her down to him with so much force that she lost all balance and fell heavily against him. She might have been warned by the glitter in his eyes. He grasped her shoulders through the black mesh of her hair, not caring if he hurt her. She caught her breath and the blood pounded in her ears.

It was too late and resistance was beyond her. He bent his dark head and found her mouth, forcing it open with flagrant punishing mastery. Multiple piercing sensations shot through her and a frightening loss of identity. The world she knew fell away from her and there was only Guy, the male scent of him, his lean length, the strength and the mastery, the questing mouth that was forcing the very heart from her body.

She heard herself make a queer little sound that was half a sob and then she was free of him, but only for a moment. She swayed giddily, her head drooping, but he swooped and held her wrists, his grip making her catch her breath.

"So the grand manner has begun to collapse a little?" Then more gently, as if in an afterthought, "Just how long did you think you could pull off all that fiery backchat? Next time you'll remember it's a direct invitation to disaster."

Excitement, anger, humiliation exploded in her head with a dull reddish glare. She tried to pull away from him, but he was holding her hands. She was on fire now with the urgent need to retaliate somehow.

His dark eyes lingered on her full, quivering mouth.

"You want mercy, don't you, but you can't be sure I deal in the gentler virtues. In fact, as you've told me once too often, I don't." He forced her to hold up her head. "If you insist in kindling a blaze, my little cat, you can hardly complain if you get scorched yourself."

At last she had her hand free. It flew through the air, to be caught and imprisoned again. Guy laughed at her predicament. "Perhaps this will serve to reduce your childish tantrums to the insignificance they deserve. It's time you grew up, my little Karen."

She tried to turn her head away, but the effort was futile, and then she was incapable of all further action, a fever of excitement entering her bloodstream. Her youth, inexperience, her headlong physical response to him, undreamed of in all her lifetime, combined against her. For the first time in her life, Karen surrendered to a force too big for her to handle and fainted dead away.

When she opened her eyes she was lying on her own bed, her hand upflung as though to shield her gaze from his turbulent dark vitality. Her soft sensuous mouth quivered with emotional imbalance. She turned her face away, a tear rolling back to fall on to the gorgeous print of the bedspread.

"For God's sake don't cry!" he said tersely. "I've had enough! You're the most volatile child, so highly strung I'm not even sure you're tame. Yet those very qualities are part of your attraction." He came towards the bed, turning up her face to him. His hand brushed back her hair with a kind of subdued violence.

"Now what's happened to all that wonderful repartee? It's quite a job keeping up with your emotional vagaries."

The tiny bodice of her gown moved with her accelerated heartbeats. Something flickered in his night-black eyes. She gazed back at him speechlessly, her golden irises shimmering with a surfeit of emotion.

"Relax, child. You over-extend your emotional capital like no one I know." His glanced leaped over her. "I had the certain premonition you'd be trouble the first time I saw you again in Melbourne." His voice was unbearably cynical. "But you've no need to fear any more dishonourable advances, they won't be forthcoming. I think I've accomplished all I intended – to jar you out of your dream state." He flicked away a tear with a half tender, half impatient gesture. "Get out of that dress and into bed. Nothing and no one will seem quite so bad in the morning. Even me."

He moved to the door and Karen found her voice. It sounded oddly light, even far away to her ears.

"That's the first time I've ever fainted," she said wonderingly. "The first time I've ever been kissed ... against my will ... and I *hated* it !" She impelled herself upwards, half reclining on her elbow.

Guy cut her off brutally. "Your reactions, my contrary little cat, were quite unmistakable. I could make love to you now and you wouldn't even fight me ... after the first minute."

Her black, silver-sheened head on its slender neck was tilted towards him, poetic, pre-Raphaelite. His dark masculinity was an intolerable stimulant, but she was determined to hold his gaze. She stared back at him, unable to control a slight trembling.

"Oh, but I *would* !" she murmured with passionate vehemence. His eyes, black and ironic, swept over her and with no intention of will Karen crumpled over on the bed and softly and helplessly began to cry, the longing of Eve upon her.

Guy was silent, but only for a minute. "A cry won't hurt you," he observed unfeelingly. "It might even be chastening. Pleasant dreams, little spitfire," he added, and shut the door with finality.

CHAPTER VI

In the weeks that slipped by, one by one, since the party, Karen found herself adjusting to a multi-faceted household that still managed to present to the outsider an impression of unity. To her great relief, Philip was fully integrated, a pound or two heavier and the constant shadow of Mark Amber, to whom he was devoted.

Karen's own relationship with Mark and Patricia Amber was at once and completely — family. Though it would have grieved her to put it into words, she found in her mother's cousin and closest girlhood companion the very qualities she had looked for and found wanting in her mother. It was strange. It was ironic, but it was true! She had come predisposed to be on her guard against the Ambers, to see through their surface charm and glitter, but daily contact made aloofness an exercise in futility. Patricia Amber was, as her brother had insisted, a wonderful woman.

Guy, of course, was Guy; a man of immense charisma. He came and went, a rocket on their horizon, but once and for all the centrifugal force around whom the household revolved. That his prolonged absences often coincided with Celia's overnight stays in town Karen not for a moment put down to coincidence. She was young, but she wasn't naïve. Yet the knowledge that Celia Amber saw her brother-in-law as her own special possession was as oppressive as a heavy coat in the middle of summer.

Celia was, Karen soon discovered, the complete butterfly and on this account a fascinating psychological study: for Celia Amber was devoted — to herself. Her preoccupation with her looks, her clothes, her figure, her extraordinary diet régime was perhaps understandable in a glamorous, much photographed woman, and certainly the results were quite wonderful. Celia Amber, with care, wealth and great determination, was preserving an astonishing aura of youth.

She knew everyone who was anyone and was often photographed with a great many of them. No major event on the social scene was complete without her. Her beauty, her family connections and her fabulous clothes easily secured her an entrée. She had a penthouse apartment in town where she would stay for days in a row and often bore Liane off with her. But to Karen, Celia had little to say.

When she was at Belle Amber she breakfasted each morning in bed. Karen often saw Marie, the little household help, carry a silver breakfast tray up to Celia's suite. She noticed with wry amusement the delicate lace mat, the fragile china, the pink, dew-drenched rosebud — never the full flower — jostling the grapefruit juice in the tall, frosted glass, the slivers of dry toast and the silver pot of strong black coffee. Then around about eleven, Celia descended — to the lower orders, as Rikki put it, exquisitely dressed for luncheon, or a bridge party or whatever; her hat, her dress, her accessories perfection. These were the weapons of conquest and they were the best on the market. Long after she left, her perfume subtly pervaded the atmosphere — a vivid reminder that Celia Amber wanted the best things out of life and was getting them!

When Liane was at home she was charming. She was friendly and sought Karen's company, but so much of her conversation revolved around her mother — Celia's lovely hair, her lovely clothes, her fabulous taste, the men who were in love with her, that Karen found it hard to evince interest. Liane was too firmly tied by the fabled silver cord, and Karen was always thankful when Rikki came along to infuse a little conflict into the conversation or a new, badly needed topic of interest. Neither of Celia Amber's children could strike the happy medium with regard to their mother. To Liane she was the sum of perfection. To Rikki — a fallen angel!

Towards the end of the month Guy flew interstate for a trade convention, leaving the whole household to bear the *ennui* of his absence. At once Celia took off for town, ostensibly to face the long wearisome hours of dress fittings. With the holiday season ahead, she explained, one simply couldn't appear in the "same old rags". This statement Karen found ludicrous. Celia Amber in rags would turn the whole town out, she thought waspishly.

Karen's own routine went on as before. She got Pip off to school, completed the few household tasks she had taken over from Aunt Patricia and in the time remaining before lunch she usually practised. Often Aunt Patricia would slip into the room to listen, her dark head with its thick chignon coming to rest against a wing-backed chair. A dreamy, abstracted expression would play over her fine, sensitive face, for she was an appreciative listener. Sometimes when Karen finished playing she would surprise a curious attitude on the part of the older woman. Aunt Patricia would start as if awakening from a sleep and look intently into Karen's face as if in search of something, and a little shiver would run down Karen's spine. It seemed to her then that the expression in the luminous dark eyes was faintly tragic. But the expression never lasted for more than an instant and everything was normal and relaxed again.

Aunt Patricia was a wonderful companion. She was quiet and contemplative when one felt inclined that way, yet she loved to talk. She would tell Karen about the places she had visited: Paris, London, Rome, Madrid and Vienna, the Americas and the South Africa that she loved: the books she had read. She liked to talk also about the theatre – plays and ballet and music – but the only thing she never talked about was love. Karen found this curious and faintly intriguing.

In her forties, Patricia Amber was still a beautiful woman and she must have been very lovely as a girl. Better still, she had a warm and generous nature, the true womanly qualities that endured. Yet she had never married! Never apparently had a serious love affair and if she had, she never spoke of it, nor had it amounted to anything. Her parents' broken marriage would have affected her, made her more cautious, but it didn't really explain anything. Patricia Amber, in her own way, was an enigma!

One particular afternoon when she felt at a loose end, Karen went in search of Mark Amber. She found him in the library, occupying the tan leather armchair behind the great desk of mahogany. He looked up vaguely, recognition flooding his eyes.

"I didn't hear you, my dear. You just drifted in like Trish's lilacs." His lively dark eyes twinkled under his tufted brows. He pushed away a great sheaf of papers. "I was just getting bogged down anyway. Come over." Karen smiled and walked over to the desk. "May I see?"

"Of course." He spoke without hesitation, inviting her interest.

Karen picked up a large photograph from a scattered pile of them. It was a picturesque stone building with shutters over the windows and a leaf-filled pond in front of it.

"What's this beautiful place?" she asked with interest.

Mark Amber slid his glasses back on his nose. "Show me. Ah yes, the wine cellar at Groot Constantia near Cape Town. The vineyard was planted in the 1680s by Governor Van der Stel. I took that shot – oh, let me see now, about five years ago."

"That's Guy, of course, in the corner. Isn't it?" What a ridiculous question, she thought, a little annoyed with herself for asking. It couldn't be anyone else with that splendid dark head.

Mark Amber gave the photograph another casual glance. "Yes, that's Guy. He didn't know he was in it. We went together – a most beautiful place. Dutch domestic architecture was at its zenith in those days. I would say the old buildings are every bit as beautiful as those we found in Europe. The Constantia valley at the back of Table Mountain is a sight to behold, probably one of the richest valleys in the world. I hope you'll see it one day."

Karen smiled and picked up another photograph. "I hope so too. And who is this distinguished old gentleman with the whiskers? One of the Ambers?" Her eyes danced into light.

Mark Amber clicked his tongue in mock reproach. "My dearest child, such ignorance for a member of the family! That distinguished gentleman is James Busby — some say the founder of our wine industry, an Englishman like my own grandfather and a real original. He was sent out as headmaster to an orphanage at Cabramatta and lost no time at all introducing viticulture to the student curriculum."

"Heavens, he *was* an original!" Karen had a graphic mental picture of the scene.

A smile crossed Mark Amber's face and was gone. "Well, the idea was to support the orphanage with the profits and incidentally to teach the orphans a trade. He succeeded quite well at both."

"Now I remember," Karen hit on some latent knowledge. "He was the first man to publish a textbook on viticulture in the southern hemisphere."

"Now you're on the track! James Busby performed an invaluable service for his adopted country, touring the French vineyards at the request of the British Government and collecting over twenty thousand cuttings of *cépages nobles*. Today, of course, those same vines are protected by law. Export of cuttings is illegal. But fortunately for us, the French vignerons at that time were generous with their vines and advice. It's only in our own time that the French have been forced into keeping their knowledge and their noble vines to themselves. The competition is ferocious and too much business has already been lost to Australia and the Cape. Yet it took less than a century for the vine to conquer our own land and provide us with a major industry and our own family and the countless families that work for us with our life's blood. I only wish my dear grandfather could see our immense population of vines. The sight would gladden his heart ... the culmination of his dreams! All our wonderful vineyards ... Coonawarra, Great Western, North and Central Victoria, the Hunter Valley, our own foothills and Southern Vales and the beautiful Barossa Valley. You've seen the Barossa, haven't you? I know Stephen had family connections there."

Karen smiled. "Yes, years ago, Uncle Mark, when Father was alive. We went up for the Barossa Vintage Festival. I still remember the choirs and the bands, the grape picking, the tastings, the judging. The Valley seemed to me then unlike any other part of Australia."

"And so it is, with little German settlements all over the place ... quite old world, continental. We have a lot of migrant families working for us at Ambervale, and their pruning ability is something to see. Grape pruning, as you know, is one of the arts of wine, along with cultivation and cellar technique. Some men are born pruners, some never learn. There has to be this special feeling for the needs of each individual vine, you see. Severe pruning can result in poor quality wine while light, right pruning tends to produce high quality wine. Our workers are renowned for their skill and sensitivity."

"But the trade goes back far beyond our own experience, doesn't it, Uncle Mark?"

"Well, yes, for the most part. Our immigrants came from viticultural Europe, familiar with and trained to the vines of Europe. We had a head start, as you might say. Then too, the gold rush of the 1850s provided us with scores of vinearoons. Disappointed gold prospectors from all over the world turned to planting vineyards, especially in Victoria ... English, Swiss, French, German. Take your own family, my dear. The Hartmann winery of your grandfather's day produced an outstanding red. I remember it well; a complex perfume, distinctive style and an excellent grip in the finish. We owe a great deal to our migrants. Indeed, Baron du Pury and the Castella brothers produced the great Lilydale Yerings. Classic wines of Australia, comparable with the wines of France's golden age."

Karen's frown was regretful. "They aren't in existence any longer, are they?"

"A million pities, no. Our dairying industry has taken over at the expense of our wonderful côtes. A tragedy for the vigneron, but there you are!"

Karen looked to the mound of closely written foolscap.

"How is your own work progressing?"

"Not as fast as I could wish. Some days I just seem to dither like Dagwood. Getting old, I suppose."

"Never that." Karen looked at the silver hair that still sprang back thickly from the fine brow, and smiled. "Who does your typing?" she asked in her musical voice.

"Guy's secretary handles everything for me, my dear. Any one of the girls in the typing pool does it, I imagine."

Karen hesitated, but only for a second. "Would you like me to help you, Uncle Mark? I'm quite a good typist and I'd be happy to help out. I've so much free time on my hands with Pip at school. Next year I must get a job, no matter what Guy says. I'm not really a lady of leisure, you know. It's agin my nature!" she smiled at him, showing her small, pretty teeth.

"Are you serious, my dear?"

"Perfectly!" she assured him.

Mark Amber whipped off his glasses. "Well, really I don't know what to say. It would be the ideal arrangement so far as I'm concerned. As it is now, I have to be careful with my longhand, make it perfectly legible, and that in itself is an ordeal, I can tell you. But with *you* in the house! ... and you're a typist?" He looked at her with renewed admiration.

"Well then, it's settled."

"On one condition. I pay you a wage."

Karen lost her smile.

"Good grief, I'm on more than adequate allowance now. Guy simply ignores all my protests as though they don't exist."

Mark Amber smiled.

"That would be Guy, and you have a surprising way of speaking your mind. However, a wage, dear, otherwise I wouldn't consider it. I'm not exactly down to my last three-penny bit, you know."

"Very well, then. I must say I feel happy about it. Like Pip, I feel I've so much to learn. It will be quite an experience for me."

"Well now, let's be businesslike, seeing we're *in* business. How about two hours a day, starting next Monday? Your time-table will be quite elastic. I know how much Trish enjoys your company and you practice in the mornings. I've some wonderful things to show you as well. Luke and I picked them up in our travels when we were boys."

"I don't remember Uncle Luke," Karen said carefully, a flicker of expression crossing her face.

Mark Amber's eyes leapt into life, the deep grooves in his cheeks pronounced.

"Lionhearted, my brother. A lion of a man, tremendously vital. There couldn't be two of him."

Karen's eyes suddenly stung. She sensed what he might be feeling and was moved.

Mark Amber contemplated a spot on the ceiling.

"Richard's death finished him off. Though it was as well Luke died, he would have made an intolerable invalid. Intolerable for him, intolerable for us all to have to watch him brought down; a vigorous man no longer whole. He adored the children, though it was always Guy who was closest to him. Richard was a little like Julia, his mother, you know."

"No one ever seems to mention Aunt Julia."

"No, dear, perhaps not. Trish and Guy feel a degree of disappointment in their mother. Perhaps they feel she let their father down. There was the divorce, of course. They never were suited, though Julia was very pretty as a girl. But with such reserve! I often wonder how they got together in the first place. Julia couldn't stand the life — a handsome, vital, increasingly successful husband, an expanding business, the demands on Luke's time, the increasing social obligations her position imposed on her. Some women would lap it up, Celia for one, but Julia just seemed to fold up under it."

"She remarried, didn't she?"

"Yes, an American. Writer fellow. They live in the States, California. Trish and Guy usually call on her once or twice a year. I believe she's quite happy." His expression was turned inwards, impassive, remote.

"Misalliances," Karen said sadly.

"Yes, dear. One grows, the other stays still or grows in another direction. I often think Trish and Guy have been affected to a certain extent. Women have been hurling themselves at Guy's head, to my knowledge, since he's been in his teens, and Trish was always a beautiful girl, yet neither of them are married. Much too cautious, I'd say! I've even tried to chat Guy up about it, after all he has a responsibility as head of the family, but he just laughs it off. He tells me he'll 'know her when he sees her' and damn it all, he's thirty-five! You'd think he'd have seen her by now."

"Perhaps she *has*!" Karen said very dryly, then recollected herself. She had not meant to say that. The words presented themselves, unbidden.

Instant comprehension flared in the still bright eyes.

"No, my dear, that would never do. Now why is it you induce me to talk? Unless it's those great golden eyes." He changed the subject abruptly. "Now what say I run you in to pick up Pip this afternoon? It's much too hot for him to walk from the bus. You don't drive, do you, my dear, though I think perhaps you're about to. Guy was only saying about sending a car out for you."

"A car?" Karen looked her bewilderment. "He didn't say anything at all to me."

"Well now, that's his way. Guy's been making a lot of decisions since he's been little more than a boy. Add that to a naturally autocratic disposition and there you are! Guy's a lot like Luke, and that's saying something!"

Karen said nothing at all. What was there to say, anyway? A naturally autocratic disposition! She couldn't agree more!

CHAPTER VII

THE car was delivered the same afternoon Guy returned from Interstate; a four-cylinder Torana with a metallic bronze paint finish and a plush vinyl interior to match. Karen was torn between a feeling of excitement and pure outrage. Every minute of the day her independence was being usurped. She could just feel her defences crumbling bit by bit. No one seemed to appreciate her dilemma. Aunt Trish merely patted her arm with a fond "How nice," Pip pronounced himself thrilled and promptly buried his nose, like a puppy, in the wonderful-smelling upholstery and Uncle Mark offered to give her driving lessons. Only Celia and Liane, who were rarely at home with the endless round of social commitments, were not available for comment. Rikki, blinded perhaps by his expected fortune, couldn't hit on the right note either.

Standing in the drive admiring the car, despite herself Karen annnounced quite bitterly: "This is the ultimate humiliation! I feel like a garlanded calf. I'm quite sure Guy would put a ring through my nose if he felt like it, and what's more he'd expect me to wear it."

"Now what are you on about?" Rikki's blond head emerged from an examination of the woodgrain dash. "You're quite a card, Karo. You'll need a car — run Pip about and all that! What's a car here or there to Guy? He's got three himself. You have to admire how he handles our affairs. You've just got to see things in perspective, kiddo. You're not on your own now. You have a family and thank your lucky stars you can dig deep in the old coffers. Now hop in and we'll go for a burn."

Karen hopped in, still grumbling. After a few minutes it occurred to her that "burn" was the operative word. Rikki drove in short furious bursts more suited to a Grand Prix, she

118

thought edgily. Certainly he had control of the car, but Karen began to feel a certain proprietorial interest in its paintwork. After all, it was brand new!

Outside the tall wrought iron gates at the end of the drive Rikki reversed the car and pulled over on the grass.

"Change places, kiddo."

"My first lesson?"

"Nothing less. Come on now, don't look so morose. Driving is a piece of cake, nothing to it. Even young Pip could do it – with his eyes closed, by the look of him."

Karen hesitated. "I don't think I can. Not today, Rikki. I feel like I've got banana legs. I just could hit something."

Rikki patted her shoulder. "Never fear, my little pal. I'll keep my fingers crossed for you till they ache."

"Well, I'll try it, but this time without the wisecracks."

Rikki continued to be facetious, showing a fine contempt for the elementary principles of driver training. A quick run down on the dash, the gears and the pedals, and Karen was expected to take off.

"Through the gates?" she asked, swallowing visibly.

"I don't see why not. They're as big as a mountain."

She put the car in gear with no trouble at all, but unfamiliar with clutch control, made the car buck like a brumby colt, though mercifully it cleared the tall pillars.

"God save us all!" Rikki uncovered his eyes. "You can put your foot down now, dear. Second gear, that's it. You've got it! There's been that much improvement, at any rate."

Karen put her foot down. "Go and soak your head! What next, master mind?"

"I'll think of something," Rikki promised. "When you're up to twenty, change to third gear. You do *steer* nicely, dear," he pointed out kindly as she narrowly missed quite a large rock to the side of the drive.

Karen threw him a long, unfriendly look. "Take a week's notice, starting last week. I don't wish to appear ungrateful or unappreciative, but you're a lousy driving instructor. Shouldn't all this be explained to me from a stationary position? I mean I've had pupils myself, you know!" The car, following the direction of her eyes, travelled towards the embankment.

"God, not there!" Rikki sat bolt upright with a jerk and straightened the wheel. "It's a fair old jump from there." Carefully he eased himself back into his seat. "Not cottoning on to this too quickly, are you, love? Still, you *look* gorgeous. That yellow dress — it's wonderful! You keep coming at me like a Van Gogh sunflower. Now pull up over there and start off again. Get the feel of the clutch, if you can. It can't be too different from pedalling a piano."

"It's quite different, I assure you!" So complete was Karen's concentration, she missed first gear and the car shot into reverse. On the edge of her panic she could hear Rikki yelling: "The brake, girl, the brake! Hit the brake. For God's sake, I haven't even shown you reverse!"

Sick and shaken by the speed of the car, Karen finally got her foot off the accelerator. She brought the car to a halt well off the drive and heading for the trees.

Rikki was looking at her with honest perplexity. "'Struth, sweet, you worry the gears like a terrier worries an old shoe! Just what were you going for?"

Karen's sense of humour reasserted itself. "First, believe it or not." Her legs felt awfully wobbly. "I've had enough for today, Rikki. I haven't got the hang of it, and if you'll forgive my saying so you're a shocking teacher. All this drive as you go, and sunflowers coming at you ... the trees were coming at us, more like it!"

Rikki leant over and switched off the ignition, pulling on the handbrake. "You could be right, love. I'm more at one with the flowering world and the nesting birds. Besides, I'd like to make love to you."

He was not laughing now but serious, with the "little boy", slightly wilful expression, she remembered.

"You've got a lovely mouth, Karo," he said dreamily, "and the mouth reveals the personality, so they say."

Karen smiled. "Thanks for something! I've almost no morale left. Now, any better ideas?"

Rikki's eyes shone with a sudden light. "Give me time, kiddo." He leant over and pulled her towards him. "Kiss me, you glorious dimwit."

"No!"

"Yes. I've been hanging on the vine long enough." His voice was insistent. The sun turned the silver-gilt hair to a glory and Karen glanced at him appreciatively through half-closed lids.

"You're very easy on the eye, Rikki."

He smiled at her lazily. "I admire your taste."

"Even so, I'm afraid I'll have to ask you to be platonic."

"God, nothing that drastic!" Rikki's eyes were fastened longingly on her full, moulded mouth. It tilted suddenly.

"Oh, all right!" She leaned forwards and ran her mouth across his cheek, a caress as delicate as a butterfly's wing. Rikki's hands tightened on her, long-fingered and very strong.

"You provoking little devil! How dare you insult my manhood? Just remember you're only a very commonplace set of chemicals."

There was a slight scuffle broken up by the unmistakable sound of a car horn. It was the Jaguar, coming up the drive — and fast. Their heads spun as one.

Guy swung the big car up behind them and got out, moving over the sloping ground with long, easy strides. He cleared his throat delicately, his dark eyes alive with all the dynamic energy that was so vitally a part of him.

"Am I intruding on some sort of crisis?" he inquired smoothly, flicking a sardonic, half amused eye over their young, upflung faces. "What's this? Deserts of silence?"

"That's blown it sky-high!" Rikki fell back against the seat, his eyes closed in disgust.

Guy's mouth twitched. "And how are you, little one? In

121

the middle of a lesson?"

"End of one," Rikki supplied laconically. "If I'm to die I prefer to do it by my own hand."

Karen turned on him, her eyes huge with protest. "I never realised you could be such a traitor!"

"Joke, dear," Rikki reassured her, then sat up quickly. "I have it, suddenly and completely! Guy will teach you. He's the ideal man in a crisis. Fearless ... unflappable ... This kind of thing is against all my principles. Where there's danger Richard is always first to quit the field. I might look a tough nut, but I'm jelly inside."

Karen's high-spirited face was beginning to flash fire. "Your wit isn't affecting me at all today, Rikki."

He merely grinned, his eyes on Guy. "Getting a bee in her bonnet, is she?"

Guy smiled and looked at Karen. "My time is very short!"

"That's what I thought myself," she said huffily.

He seemed to reconsider. "Now let's see. I can think of a dozen different solutions ... all equally impossible."

Karen shot him a dazzling topaz glance. "This is getting us nowhere." She began to move her head fretfully from side to side in nervous dissatisfaction. "I never wanted a car in the first place. I don't even want to learn how to drive."

"Karo, love!" All at once Rikki sounded contrite, stabbed by the slight break in her voice. Guy merely laughed and opened the car door and pulled her out to him.

"Don't you know when you're being teased, my lamb? It's an old Amber habit. You're not bad at it yourself."

She looked up at him with a mixture of emotions, feeling herself at a disadvantage. His hand closed over her collarbone with its now familiar caressing movement of the thumb. She expelled a long breath and tossed her black hair over her shoulder in uneasy fascination.

"You bring out the worst in me, Guy, and that's a fact!"

"Did you think I was unaware of it?"

Rikki looked from one to the other, his eyes narrowing against the sun. "Exit Sir Galahad on his way to the Holy Land."

Guy gave a brief laugh. "I take it you're going to stable the car. Thanks, Rick. We'll defer lessons until tomorrow when I have more time."

"The urgency's not that extreme," Karen bit out, barely able to contain herself at such patronage.

Guy glanced at her haughty young face reprovingly. "Don't you want to thank me in that wonderfully individual manner of yours?"

"I think she does," Rikki volunteered. "Right-oh, people, I think I'll have a drink before the boat sails." He swung the car back on to the drive, making short work of clearing the bend in the drive. Karen looked after him with new-found admiration. Surely if Rikki could do it, so could she!

"That's what I call magnificent panache," she murmured wistfully. "I don't think I can be mechanically minded."

Guy looked philosophical and took her arm to put her into his car. "It's not as hard as it looks, though a couple of minor points do occur to me. One is — kissing on the job! It's apt to weaken a beginner's concentration."

"Kissing?" Karen's slanting brows shot up incredulously. Did he ever miss anything?

"That's what I said. Doesn't it strike you as a trifle unusual for the first lesson?" He looked into her flushed face then held the point of her chin. "With no effort from you, my pet, you could knock Rikki for six, and that would never do. I don't believe in early alliances."

Karen gave an audible gasp. "You're a dead ringer for Cesare Borgia! I don't think I've ever encountered such proud authority."

His voice slowed to a drawl. "Try to hold your enthusiasm in check, my pet. I merely passed a remark. You and Rick are my responsibility. Neither of you is twenty-one yet. Besides, no good could come of anything there, my girl."

She tossed her wilful dark head. "Why don't you add – mark my words!"

"Mark my words!" Guy obliged weightily, and suddenly laughed, his teeth very white in his tanned face.

Just as suddenly Karen's resentment crumpled like so much tissue paper. That smile was unfairly devastating, creasing his lean cheeks, whirling her into danger.

"Now why is it you always make me feel there's a war on and I'm right in the middle of it?"

His eyes were on the pure curve of her throat. "Maybe because you're such a *female* female. You want to be dominated, but you insist on fighting it every inch of the way."

"Do I?" she smiled at him. "I think I'm frightened."

"Well, it's damned well time. Now tell me, how do you like the car? I didn't think you'd want anything bigger, not at this stage, anyway." He brushed his knuckle against her cheek-bone. "Turn your head this way and say thank you. With practice it may come a little easier."

"It will have to, won't it?" Her mouth curved and her eyes tilted deepening with colour. Guy's face altered and she drew in her breath sharply, filled with the wildest notion that he meant to kiss her. She couldn't bear it. Not in broad daylight when she was so defenceless. Instinctively she arched away from him, without the slightest weapon.

Guy regarded her manoeuvres coolly. "I never make the same mistake twice, my pet."

Karen ran the tip of her tongue over her top lip. Her efforts to appear casual fell hopelessly flat.

"I'm sure no one can ever remember your making the *first* one."

He laughed. "God, you've got a kick like a contrary mule!"

She could smile at him now, the bad moment over. "Now how is that possible?"

Lazily Guy moved his hand from the back of the seat to her white nape. "If we ever do have a confrontation, little one, I promise you Vesuvius will seem a mere bagatelle compared to it."

She kept her head up, her eyes clear and direct. "That's the *dear* thing about you, Guy. You're so tolerant!"

He shook her then, none too lightly, and her head lolled like a flower on its slender stalk. "If it will please you," she mocked him, "from now on I'll tremble when you frown."

His brilliant dark gaze was ironic. "How prettily you lie! Sometimes you act as much nine as nineteen."

She sighed. "If that's the case, I give up."

"That's all right. You just give up." He released her with a quick grin. "Besides, it's already been ordained that I should influence your life."

"Don't say another word!" Karen warned him. "I won't listen!" A subtle excitement began to stir in her.

His eyes glittered tauntingly in her handsome dark face.

"Don't be so melodramatic, my orchid. You'll listen if I want you to."

Karen turned her head away, a restraint upon her, unspoken but very real. It was dangerous to get too close to Guy, yet perversely she was hopelessly drawn to a man who could only hurt her, a man worlds removed from her in experience and sophistication. She would have to steel herself against his masterful ways.

Guy leaned forward and switched on the ignition and Karen allowed herself one glance at his dark profile. She was trembling a little at his nearness. He turned his head swiftly, pinning her gaze, and the look in his night-dark eyes told her quite plainly that he was fully aware of her predicament.

Karen sat back and followed the line of the poplars with her eyes. More than anything she wanted to be alone. She was disturbed and alerted now to anything that might lie beneath the surface. To yearn for the impossible was little short of insanity!

CHAPTER VIII

It was Aunt Patricia who suggested that Karen and Liane spend a day in town before Pip started his holidays. Perhaps lunch and a show, she mentioned over breakfast, and thus innocently set off a chain of events that were to draw into line the inevitable antagonists – Karen and Celia.

It all started off harmlessly enough. The day was crisp and beautiful with an air of complete normality; the open enjoyment and laughing during the drive to the city, their giggling search for a parking space big enough for Karen to back the car in with any degree of safety, all lent strength to Karen's feeling that this was going to be a good day.

Lunch was a hilarious affair, partially due to the not one but two unaccustomed cocktails that preceded it, with Liane laughing helplessly at Karen's more outrageous *bons mots*. Afterwards it was Liane who suggested they take in a main feature film of the glossy variety – not one Karen would have picked on herself, but she went along happily, infected by the younger girl's high spirits.

In the near cold dimness of the theatre Karen decided that only one thing saved the film from being consigned to the garbage can – the presence of the anti-heroine, a tall, good-looking brunette, who bore a marked physical resemblance to Liane – or rather, to a Liane dressed to type. Karen was thoroughly intrigued. She sat to attention and prodded Liane in the ribs.

"That's you!"

Liane looked blank. "Who?"

"That dishy type up there."

Liane looked back at the screen, but the "Ssh!" from behind them silenced all further conversation. Karen's fertile brain was evolving a plan. She sat there isolated in her dream world, churning it over. A complete change of hairstyle was the focal point of the plan. It would make the world of difference to Liane's appearance. With Liane's celluloid double up there on the screen she could hardly fail to miss that. But how did one go about instant transformation? Liane's short bubble cut didn't lend itself to adaptation. It would be ages before it would grow out to a length.

A wig, of course! It was the obvious and simple solution. Everyone was wearing one. The more Karen thought about it the better the idea seemed. The interval couldn't come soon enough! She sat on, bored stiff with all the unintentional parody and the radiantly amoral female lead.

Even in the post-theatre dazzle of sunshine Karen's enthusiasm was unabated. Liane, only eighteen, for all her look of ripe young maturity, was easily talked into the experiment. In the exclusive wig boutique she drank in her reflection like a lost soul at a waterhole.

"Hello, Cleopatra!" Karen said mischievously, her piquant eyes alight with admiration.

"Is this really me?"

Karen grinned. "Didn't I tell you a fringe would suit you? It really is a super wig, and the colour match is perfect. You can't tell the difference from your own hair. Luckily you're tall enough to wear that style beautifully."

"But a wig!" Liane was twirling this way and that, not quite crediting the transformation.

"Oh, go on! All the glamour girls have a whole wardrobe of wigs and hair-pieces. Don't tell me Gina Holmes didn't have one on at the party."

"She must have," Liane said thoughtfully. "She was a blonde at the afternoon parade. I do look rather nice, don't I?"

"You know darned well you do. Remarkably chic, like a cover on *Vogue* magazine. You've got good bones, like Aunt Trish."

"I'm not beautiful like Trish," Liane said simply.

"You will be." Karen spoke with such finality that Liane took heart from it. "Now, what about some new clothes to go with the new image?"

Liane smiled. "Why not?"

"Why not indeed? You're not hampered by a depressing bank balance."

In the stores Liane bought magnificently. In that respect at least, she was the image of her mother. Karen, who was used to going from store to store comparing merchandise and prices, was both amused and awed. Liane swept through departments with "charge it" and "put it on my account", and saleswomen, with an eye to commission, charged her, deserting their less profitable customers. It was "Good afternoon, Miss Amber. How are you, Miss Amber? We have some wonderful new styles, Miss Amber . . . just come in . . . too too lovely . . . just you, in fact."

They weren't in the least like Liane, Karen thought, and the flattery was outrageous. Her eyes sparkled and she looked across at Liane, expecting to encounter a matching twinkle, but Liane seemed completely unaware of it. This was the same fulsome attention she had received all her life.

They had a wonderful time! Liane gave Karen *carte blanche* in choosing the various outfits, perhaps as a reward for hitting on the idea of the wig. In the clothes that suited her, with her shoulders held back and her head high, Liane revealed a svelte figure and a lovely long length of thigh. By the time they were through, both girls were flushed and excited and the admiring glances they received over coffee had the effect on Liane of rain on a desert flower. She blossomed astonishingly, her cheeks full of unwonted colour.

Their high spirits lasted all the way back to Belle Amber and Karen felt a special thrill in being able to bring about such a change. More remarkable than anything was the transformation in Liane's posture. She was walking with free, swinging movements, tossing her black, glossy mane. Her dark

128

eyes under the thick straight fringe held a new self-awareness and there was a look of competence and forthrightness about her. Karen regarded her with warmth and affection. The family were in for a few surprises!

As it happened, the girls were the ones to be surprised. Laughing and chattering just inside the entrance hall, they were greeted by Aunt Trish coming through to meet them. Her eyes registered her instant approval of the metamorphosis. She opened her mouth to comment, but was arrested by the sound of small high-arched feet, tapping their way down the staircase. They all looked up simultaneously.

Celia was coming on down the stairs, creamed and perfumed and dressed to perfection, smoothing her gloves over her fragile wrists. At the first sight of the two girls she stood transfixed, then gave a curious, high-pitched squeal. Instantly Rikki appeared in the hallway.

"What was that?"

His aunt answered him. "Nothing, dear."

"God, I thought it was a train heading for a level crossing!"

Celia paid no attention to her son. Her eyes were all for her daughter.

"My dearest child!" the sweet voice held the crack of a whip. "You look positively eye-catching ... *gaudy* ... and what is that *thing* you have on your head?"

Rikki reeled in his tracks. "Oh, the selfless shining love of a mother! A heart as big as the world!" He gave his sister a long earnest glance. "You look terrific, kid. One hell of a good-looking girl, not a carpet to be trampled on. Your idea, Karo?"

Celia's blue eyes slanted disparagingly over the older girl. Karen felt the chill off them right to where she was standing, yet Celia maintained a rather terrifying sweetness. "How *kind* of you to take such an interest, Karen. But I do think you might have consulted me before you went rushing off. After all, I know what is best for my little girl."

Rikki threw up his hands. "This is the bloody end, as Shakespeare would say. Stick with it, kid. If you look gaudy then I'm Queen of the May." He prepared to depart. "Well, be seein' you, girls. This is no place for man or beast." He hit a hand to his chest, gazing at his sister. "My heart goes out to you in your brave fight!"

Liane looked ludicrously surprised. Used as she was to Rikki's extravagant turn of phrase, his words usually failed to register. Besides, he was always having a shot at Mother! The colour swept into her face.

"What do you think, Aunt Trish?"

"What strange modesty is this?" Patricia Amber smiled. "I think you look very stylish indeed. You can always grow your hair out. I agree with Karen and Rikki."

"But of course you do!" There was distinct malice in Celia's voice beneath the layers of sugar coating. She looked from one to the other like an exquisite Siamese kitten about to sink its little claws at the psychological moment. "I certainly don't underrate your opinion, Trish," she said sweetly, "but I do think Liane looks that teeniest bit ... *theatrical*. It would appeal to Rikki, being what he is." The sweet voice thinned with sarcasm. "Really, that boy gets odder every day!"

"Odd behaviour doesn't necessarily mean one is odd in the head," Karen burst out impetuously, her clear topaz eyes momentarily too big for the delicate oval of her face.

Celia's glance annihilated her. Karen was too tiny a pebble to cause a ripple in Celia's supreme self-confidence. Liane's face, however, was a flurry of tangled doubts which gradually resolved themselves.

"I'll go and straighten myself out," she announced listlessly, and walked up the stairs without giving her mother another glance. At the top she stared down at them for a moment, a wilted lily, with her habitual slouch.

Karen stood silently trying to hold on to her temper. She felt vaguely out of sorts with Liane. Surely Liane could have shown more spirit than that? By no stretch of the imagination could she be described as gaudy or theatrical, yet she had accepted her mother's judgment as dogma, virtually irreversible.

"Well now," Celia turned to the two silent women, her voice silky, "I'm so grateful to you, Karen. I realise now that you have a kind heart. But you *are* very young, my dear, and your taste is unformed. That's a style I don't care for Liane to copy."

"What, to look like her aunt?" Karen burst out irrepressibly, her quick temper coming to the boil.

Celia's eyes were the clear blue green of a glacier, but not half so warm. "Don't interrupt me, my dear, and don't question what I say. You're not as clever as you think you are. Also, you've got rather a malicious sense of humour. Liane didn't look in the least like Trish. *That* would have been an entirely different matter." She turned to her sister-in-law, a half smile hovering on her soft pink mouth, now that Karen was firmly reprimanded. "I must fly, Trish. Really I hadn't dreamed it was that late. I'll have to rush like mad. I'm dining with Paul Rand this evening and what with one thing and another I just know I'll look a wreck, and Paul would hate *that*!" She turned to flash an empty smile at both of them, once more on balance, in control of the situation. In her own mind at least, her malevolence was only a memory to be wielded upon occasions like a baton.

With elaborate deliberation she inspected her flawless profile in the trumeau. "That I should have a daughter with no pretension to beauty!" she murmured complacently.

The statement took Karen's breath away. "But I don't agree," she said after a minute. "Liane has enormous potential," she pointed out gallantly, "and what's more, she'll mature well!"

But Karen was tilting at windmills. Celia's glance met hers with gleaming malevolence. "Not really!" She held her voice to lightness implying that Karen's opinion was less than unimportant. "That height!" she murmured. "Liane was five feet nine when she was fifteen. Imagine!"

Patricia Amber made a convulsive protesting movement of

her hand, her dark eyes wide with distress.

"She's suffered unduly because you're so tiny."

In every way, Karen thought with fierce resentment. Celia was quite peculiar. Secure in her world of frivolity, she never stopped to count the ultimate cost of her empty successes. Wasn't obsessive behaviour symptomatic of something? But what was Celia's trouble? Why was she filling her days with endless distractions? Karen stood there milling her thoughts over.

Celia turned at last from the mirror. "Heavens, Karen, you do look fierce! Glowering would probably be the most apt term." She gave a pretty laugh. "Now be good!"

Her heels clicked, the car door slammed, then she was gone.

The two women drifted into the living room and sank down into the yielding softness of the divan. Patricia Amber's fine dark eyes were clouded and her sensitive face mirrored her mood.

"How do you stand it?" Karen spoke her thoughts aloud.

"Over the years, I've become used to it." For once Patricia was thrown off guard and the words came tumbling out. "I've come off second best to Celia for God knows how long. If I paid too much attention to her I'd find her malice clear and her every word suspect, but I've learnt to keep quiet to hold on to my loved ones. Rikki and Liane are all that is left of Richard. I love them dearly, though I could wish Liane would show a little of your spirit. If I'd antagonised Celia in the past as I've often wanted to I might have had to forfeit their company as I forfeited yours and Pip's for so long. One must tread warily with difficult natures. Occasionally I experience a great wave of indignation when I'd like to hit back as hard as I can, but my hands are tied. I simply don't know where I am. It takes another woman to fully appreciate Celia. She certainly knows her way around the men, but she has no time for her own sex. It wouldn't do for me to create friction and restraint. An armed truce is better than open conflict, I keep telling myself, but one of these days, even I'm not going to listen." Her eyes sought Karen's, pleading for understanding. "I suppose you've noticed Celia is devoted to Guy. The sun, the moon and the stars shine out of him. He's been very good to her, of course. She is, after all, our brother's widow, but Guy has lived all his life not letting his left hand know what his right hand is doing. It's his nature and his training, I suppose. I could never force him into the position where he feels he must choose between us. One thing is certain, if Celia ever becomes mistress of Belle Amber my days are numbered. Celia doesn't share her possessions. Belle Amber would be lost to me; the beloved home where we were all born. I could accept it from any other woman, but not from Celia. There's no heart to her. You've seen her with the children. She loved them when they were little, but her whole capacity for love is selfish in the last resort."

"Dear, oh dear, oh dear!" Karen was sitting mournfully looking down at her clasped hands. Stark as that summary was, she knew it was the truth.

At the sight of her young, unhappy face, warmth flowed back into Patricia's eyes. "There now, I've said too much and upset you. You're such a sensitive child, Karen, and your own life hasn't been a particularly happy one. Don't ever let anyone tell you money is everything." She smiled. "Now what say we get dressed and go out for dinner? We should be able to persuade Rikki and Lee to come with us. I don't think they're doing anything in particular."

Liane did not accompany them and in the morning she emerged from her room pale and tense with faint purple smudges under her eyes. The high gloss was completely worn off and her expensive smartness forsaken. Never had her long-legged angularity been more apparent.

The three of them sat down to the breakfast table: Karen, Liane and Rikki. Liane was staring vacantly in front of her, beating a mindless tattoo against the rim of her untouched glass of apricot juice. Without a word Karen went to the side buffet with its built-in warming plates and helped them all to eggs and bacon. The morning sun was bright in the yellow and white solarium, but the atmosphere was distinctly gloomy.

Rikki ate silently, accepting his cup of coffee from Karen in true masculine fashion, with never a word of thanks, and glancing from time to time at his sister. It took longer than Karen expected for him to whip into words.

"Well, is the reverie over?"

"What?" Liane looked up, quite startled.

"You are in a trance, dear girl. The Return of the Zombie, isn't it?"

"Knock it off, chum." Lee gave her brother a faint smile.

Rikki's face was quite sober. "Why do you do it to yourself, girl?"

"Honestly, Rikki," Liane came right out of her torpor, "some days I can't make head or tail of you! You really are an odd-ball." She looked down at her clenched hands, none too well adjusted herself.

Rikki tried again. "It's for your sake, kiddo, I'm persisting. You're very dear to me, if we must be slushy, and you did look terrific yesterday. You must know it. Ask Karo, ask Trish. Ask anyone but Mother," he groaned in a fury of impotence. "Now why isn't Guy here when we need him, damn his splendid hide?"

"You heard what *Mother* said!" Liane winced again at the memory.

"To hell with her!" Rikki shouted. "Motherhood isn't always a refining influence, you know."

"You should be ashamed ... *ashamed* !" Liane began to flare up defensively. "To speak of Mother in that fashion, and with Karen present!" Her large dark eyes glimmered with tears.

Karen was inexpressibly moved and her heart began to ache in sympathy.

"Oh, the hypocrisy of it all!" Rikki groaned, and took a great gulp of scalding coffee, then put it down with an oath. "Don't

134

you ever take any notice of anyone but darling Celia?" he bellowed, as much in pain as anything else.

"No!" Liane was tearful but unequivocal.

"You poor twisted girl," Rikki shook his head in resignation. "It's going to go hard for you, Lee." He transferred his glance to Karen. "I can't make it out. She used to get quite good grades at school, even if it was an idiot establishment for over-privileged girls."

"Oh, please!" Liane jumped to her feet, the tears falling on to her pale cheeks. Her chair went over with a crash and Karen jumped to her feet, one hand going out to the other girl. "Oh, Liane, please don't upset yourself!"

"Leave me. Leave me!" Liane tore from the room, stumbling over everything as she went.

"Do as she says," Rikki said tersely. "Leave her. She'll just have to work it out for herself. God, I feel sad," he mourned soulfully. "Sad enough to commit suicide."

Even at that moment Karen could laugh at him.

"You'll never commit suicide, Rikki – though you just could drive someone else to it," she added unkindly.

Rikki's look was reproachful. "Well, I've tried. God knows I've tried – to help, that is. But it's going to take something really big to bring Lee to her senses." His eyes glowed hotly as something occurred to him. "What about that silly twit Colin? Wouldn't you think he'd give Lee some confidence – but all he can do is rave on about Celia – isn't she *gorgeous*, fab! –" He gave a very good imitation of Colin's rather affected style. "God knows what we'll all do when Celia's a grandmother. Go underground, I suppose, or hide the poor dear babe."

Karen was growing increasingly morose. "I don't like him!"

"Who?"

"Colin!" She looked up, surprised. "I can't imagine what Liane sees in him, the conceited oaf!"

Rikki blinked. "Now that we're being frank, dear, neither can I. But Celia can, and there you are. Colin is, in his way, as malleable as Lee. There'll be no problems there. Celia can queen bee it over both households."

"I don't like him," Karen repeated herself.

"My sentiments exactly." Rikki brightened. "What say we cook up a ploy?"

Karen came back to her senses. Rikki's ploys would be predictably combustible. "Liane wouldn't thank you for it," she said with special emphasis.

Rikki desisted under her eye. "Hunger is a terrible sickness, as Pinocchio said, and I guess we're all hungry for something or someone."

Karen could only agree. But wasn't one impossible situation enough?

The next few days were grey and wet and unexpectedly cold, keeping everyone indoors, but the weekend brought stability, a hot sun and the faintest zephyr of breeze. In the light-filled studio Rikki glanced across at Karen, suddenly gay.

"That's it for today, sweetie."

"May I see?"

"Definitely not. This is all very hush-hush at the moment. Your moment will come." Rikki stood back from the easel to examine his handiwork. "Let not the spell be broken!"

"You're pleased, then?"

He merely looked at her and smiled. "I am, love. I think I've captured the essential you, that little intangible air of sadness . . . but it's frankly sensuous too."

"Well, well, how interesting!" The dreamy look left Karen's face. "Surely you haven't painted me as a voluptuous woman?"

"But you are, love," Rikki answered quite seriously. "You're coolly voluptuous and terribly sexy in the nicest possible way."

Karen made a wry little grimace. "Ugh!"

Rikki looked over at her with great penetration. "What gives with all you 'nice' puritanical women? You're all dying to be sexy, yet you all nearly faint with fright if you're accused of making the grade." He stood back and looked at the portrait. "I'm really terribly pleased with it, pet. All that lovely flawless flesh!"

Karen's face was a study. "Heavens, that talk will shift me if anything will. Flawless flesh! You talk more like the real thing every day."

"Then I take everything back, bar one thing."

"What?" Karen looked over at him suspiciously.

"You are sexy, you sweet enigmatical girl." His glance swept over her. "You know, Karo, I can't in all honesty say you'll be my last love, but you're definitely my *first*!"

"How nice of you to warn me!" Her eyes gleamed maliciously. He grinned and patted her shoulder. A good deal of their conversation followed this pattern. Impersonal — personal — always ending on a bantering note. Sometimes their talks were very serious and touched with the special melancholy that arises from youth and a rather unhappy childhood. Karen could easily read what was in Rikki's mind and she accepted the fact that Rikki, in his own way, was a little in love with her. Just as easily she accepted that Rikki would always be a little in love with a woman who fired his artistic imagination.

As for herself ever since it happened Karen carried about with her at once and for ever the memory of Guy's kiss and its profound effect on her. At regular intervals she relived it vividly. Always at the back of her mind and at the back of everything was the simple ever-present fact of her feeling for Guy. She tried to conceal it from herself and everyone else and believed that she succeeded. Except for Rikki. That would be futile. Her heart knew and she was certain Rikki knew . . . but he did not disapprove!

Rikki's voice roused her from her reverie: "What say we go for a drive this afternoon, sweetie? Seeing you *can* drive — God knows how Guy managed it," he added the essence of good will and humour.

"A systematic approach," Karen said dryly. "You said your-

137

self that Guy leaves nothing to chance. In actual fact he's an excellent teacher – witness one Karen Hartmann. We'll have to take Pip," she added matter-of-factly.

"You're joking!" Rikki's expression was ludicrous. "You can't bring the kid along. I have designs on you, don't you know? Honourable, of course."

Her smile was a masterpiece of acknowledgement and dismissal.

"I'm sorry, Rikki, but I like to give Uncle Mark a break at the weekend. Pip tires him out, so we'll take Pip. He'll be no trouble." She patted his hand consolingly. "Come and tell him now. He should be doing his homework on the sun-porch."

Pip wasn't on the sun-porch, but his homework was spread out all over the table.

"Australia is the home of *psittaciformes*?" Rikki asked with open disbelief.

"Parrots," Pip volunteered, coming back into the room, hearing voices. "Australia has the most beautiful and prolific bird-life in the world. It's my end-of-term essay. The rosellas in the garden gave me the idea. I've had a lot of fun watching them, though you have to be careful, otherwise they scoot off like greased lightning. There's the father, you see . . ."

"There always is," Rikki put in sarcastically. Pip ignored him and looked at his sister. "The father always stays behind the trunk and the mother (she's much prettier) forages around on the ground gathering grass seeds and anything she can find for the babies. Their feathers are beautiful, when the sun shines on them . . . all iridescent."

"Put in a bit about galahs," Rikki said quite kindly, gathering interest in the project. "The pink cockatoos on Grandfather Forester's property are something to see. They wheel overhead in their hundreds. It's quite a common sight in the Outback, but I never could get over it. The displays are magnificent . . . pink and silver swirling against a cobalt sky. Along the watercourses little mulga parrots gather. Just shut your eyes,

Pip, and picture a beautiful desert river winding between bizarre rose-red cliffs. All is peace and silence ... then suddenly down sweeps the bird life, flashing fire to land amongst the mulga. The lorikeets wander from region to region with the flowering trees. They swarm over the stunted mallees on the sand-plains and in midsummer when the honey starts flowing from the forest giants they literally screech to high heaven from the crown of the Karris."

"Wait, you're going too fast for me! Down sweeps the bird life ..." Pip hadn't his eyes closed at all, but was writing frantically.

"This is *your* composition," Rikki pointed out, his every word a censure.

"Gee, I'm glad you showed up," Pip replied. "I've only got a paragraph left now. On extinction ... the changing ...?" he looked at his sister.

Karen smiled and spelt it for him. "E-n-v-i-r-o-n-m-e-n-t."

Rikki looked pained. "Don't talk extinction to me, much less environment." As he sat there, Rikki, seemingly without moving his pencil was covering the page with wheeling, diving, nesting birds.

"Gee, you're clever!" Pip said admiringly.

"I am that!" Rikki agreed.

"You don't suppose ...?"

"What's that?" Rikki shot him a piercing glance.

"You don't suppose you could border my essay with birdlife? Like you're doing now?" Pip was unabashed. "I'd tell everyone it was *you*."

"That would hardly be necessary," Rikki pointed out unkindly. "These are quite exceptional drawings."

"I can draw too!" Pip announced, for the first time aggrieved.

"Right--oh." Rikki shoved the pencil at him. "Let's see you."

Pip bent his head, clamping his tongue between his teeth in concentration. He worked swiftly and Rikki looked surprised.

"A creditable effort. Here, let me show you the beak — yours is all to blazes. How do you suppose a parrot can cut through extremely hard objects? The beak, of course. Watch this, the beak is all-important." Pip moved closer. "Now don't get on top of me," Rikki warned. "I can't stand anyone breathing down my neck. It gives me the screaming heebie-jeebies. Sit down, there's a good lad !"

Karen left them to it, smiling a little. Rikki was temperamentally unsuited to imparting his knowledge with any degree of calm or civility, but already at ten, Pip had an awareness of the artistic temperament, its strengths and it limitations. When she looked back, Pip was sitting to attention, his silky dark head a respectful distance from his mentor's.

He looked up suddenly and caught his sister's eye, and his own closed on a huge wink. Karen smiled. Impressed he might have been, but overawed he was not ! She felt proud of him.

"By the way, Pip," she said smilingly, "we're going for a drive this afternoon. Be a good boy."

Rikki looked up and scowled horribly. "Are you going to scoot?"

She waggled her fingers at them. " 'Bye now !"

With the advent of the holidays, Rikki's studio now had another frequent visitor – Pip. Rikki, with unusual magnanimity and considerable pressure from Karen, had consented to allow Pip to sit quietly at a drawing board working at whatever he liked while Karen had her sitting. On these occasions a rare, companionable silence pervaded the studio. Indeed, so far as Karen was concerned it was the ideal arrangement, for then she had her small energetic brother under her nose.

The portrait was progressing smoothly, reaching its final stages. Karen alone had been permitted a glance. She was not asked her opinion, but privately thought she couldn't be that beautiful ! The countless times she had looked back at her own face, yet Rikki saw her so differently. Surely her eyes weren't that remarkable, the tilt to her eyebrows so exotic, balanced by the lovely curve Rikki had painted to her mouth. The canvas was light-charged, shimmering with clean colour, and it seemed to Karen to show tremendous promise. Rikki had experienced no difficulty at all in choosing the gown for her to sit in – the autumn leaf chiffon. One could almost reach out and grasp its gossamer softness.

The portrait showed her sitting in a gilt chair, three-quarter length, her body inclined in a fascinating attitude. Her two hands were extended, seemingly in a momentarily arrested gesture, her head on its long slender neck rising out of the creamy contours of her shoulders. It was a difficult pose, suspended animation, but Rikki demanded and got the best out of her. No matter how tiring Karen found it all, she still considered it an honour to sit for a star on the ascendant and suffered accordingly. Rikki found it nothing out of the way!

Nowadays, far from having too much time on her hands, Karen found she had very little indeed. Her work for Uncle Mark she let run over into all hours, fascinated by one man's dedication and the extraordinary saga of the sacred plant – the grapevine, with its history much longer than man's. In her thirst for even a smattering of Uncle Mark's great knowledge she often fell asleep over stories of the Bacchae in Greece, the vine's spectacular expansion through Europe, and its final world conquest in her own country. Gratified and astounded by her enthusiasm, Mark Amber had presented her with a beautiful blue *amphora* from Naples decorated with *amorini* at play among the vines. Karen loved it, but wasn't sure where to put it because she knew it was very valuable and she couldn't bear the thought of its being broken. At last she bought a small gilt wall bracket and placed it high above her head. She often lay in her bed gazing up at it, loving it, and worrying about it. But of course it never did get broken.

CHAPTER IX

THE days to Christmas ran out like sand, bringing all the things that spell Christmas to everyone, everywhere. At that time of the year, Guy was extremely busy and often stayed overnight at his town apartment, but the cards and parcels and gifts continued to stream in, delivered to the house in vanloads from friends and business connections all over the world. Even Uncle Mark was forced to concede that his work would have to be abandoned until well into the New Year.

All this time Celia and Liane flitted hither and yon. There were endless pre-Christmas functions and parties demanding their presence and they attended almost every one; the mother as fair and beautiful as a Botticelli angel, the daughter thinner, a little indifferent to what went on about her, both of them keeping messengers busy delivering enormous beribboned boxes from the leading couturiers.

As Christmas Day approached, there was only Karen and Pip to help Aunt Patricia decorate the tree. Aunt Patricia, too, received the usual windfall of invitations, but she nearly always found an excuse for avoiding each one. She couldn't have been more different from her glamorous, frivolous sister-in-law.

The Christmas tree rose to the ceiling in the living room, glittering, resplendent, hung with fragile coloured baubles that tinkled in the breeze. As they worked they sang Christmas carols and funny old songs, with Karen hitting out a few bars on the piano, laughing and joking, and once when Pip rested his dark head comfortably on Aunt Patricia's shoulder she burst into tears. Karen and Pip gazed back at her in deepest consternation, though she smiled through her tears and shrugged it all off with, "This always happens to me at Christmas. Now don't take any notice!" The moment passed and they plunged once more into merriment.

Rikki only appeared once on the scene with a sprig of mistletoe declaring with a theatrical leer that "someone is bound to fall into my trap!" But as the gaiety of the others seemed to intensify, a funny thing happened to Karen. She found herself becoming strangely dejected, depressed and unhappy. Perhaps it was because this was her first Christmas without her mother; her strange, difficult mother who had died. Though she had never understood her mother Karen missed her, and a shaft of grief for what might have been pierced her heart.

Her depression deepened, slowly, irresistibly, until one evening she had to lock herself in her room to cry her heart out. Christmas wasn't a happy time, she told herself fiercely, trying unsuccessfully to stop this paroxysm. Christmas was sad. Very sad. She fell back on the pillow again, wishing and wishing the whole festive season was over.

The tap at her door startled her. As a purely involuntary act she switched off her tears and assumed a misleadingly cheerful expression. It was probably Aunt Trish and the sight of tears would only bewilder her. Karen ran a hand over her hair, smoothed her skirt down and bit hard on her lips, colouring them the red of wild cherries.

Guy was at the door, the palest fawn of his shirt throwing his tan into stunning relief. Their eyes met and Karen obeyed a totally reckless impulse and held up her face to him.

His mouth tilted slightly and he bent his dark head and kissed the curve of her cheek. "You've been crying, darling!" His beautiful voice and the careless endearment turned her heart over. They stood close together and Karen, looking up with a kind of surprised curiosity, divined in those dark eyes a fondness for her.

Guy broke the strange silence. "Why were you crying, my little orphan?"

His perception didn't startle her. She had become used to it.

"I was sad, I suppose," she gave a wry little smile and inexplicably her mood brightened. "I'm so glad you're home again, Guy."

"You're what?" One black eyebrow shot up sardonically.

"It's no good, Guy," she said sweetly. "I refuse to cross swords with you. I've that much of the Christmas spirit."

He smiled at the odd defensiveness of her tone and she was conscious of the same old excitement. She had come to accept now, with a chronic fatalism, Guy's power to excite and disturb her. His presence focused and intensified her deepest, most complex feelings for him.

The wild illogicality of love! Her life simply wasn't her own any more, but hopelessly entangled with Guy's. His brilliant dark eyes never moved from her face. He stood, strangely silent and insistent. Under this unblinking appraisal, Karen's thoughts became wild and chaotic, the force of her emotions deepening the colour of her eyes, the most piquant feature of her beauty.

"Sadness becomes you," Guy murmured obliquely, his eyes lingering on her face and shoulders. His words overlay something he would not or could not say. His real thoughts seemed to be hidden from her, disguised by a teasing ambiguity.

Karen was jolted into speaking her thoughts aloud.

"You're the most fearfully complicated man I know!"

"Am I?"

All at once she knew this was something different. She knew it from the wild, frightened beating of her heart and the hot blood that rushed to the extremities of her body. But most of all she knew it from Guy's face.

"Guy!" she managed to get out. "Please, Guy!"

He took not the slightest notice of her, if he even heard her. He drew her against his hard, taut body and began kissing the breath out of her. He wasn't teasing any more. He was in deadly earnest.

"Please stop!" she whispered against his mouth, but he never

eemed to hear her. Suddenly all the strength left her and she let
erself be crushed up against him. Her mouth opened con-
ulsively and she clung to him ... clung to him ... her long,
huddering sigh trembling on the night air.

"Guy! ... Guy! ... Guy ...!"

Celia, on her way to her own suite, heard this strange little
moan, but could see nothing. At first her face was ludicrously
perplexed, then it froze into a fearful, unlovely mask.

She leaned against the wall, one hand going to her side, like
a woman in agony. The first surge of shock passed and she was
steadied by actuality. So it had happened! The unspeakable ...
the inevitable ... Fate reached out to everyone, everywhere ...
even to her! But Guy was hers or no one's, and by God, she
would fight for him. She continued on to her room, unnoticed.

Karen felt the first wild presentiment of disaster. She pulled
away from Guy with a kind of silent ferocity, fearful now of
this intolerable excitement, the loss of self, he engendered in
her.

"I've said you're dangerous, Guy, and you are! Cruel and
brilliant, like a ton of square-cut diamonds." She lashed out at
him, fighting for self-preservation, seeking any weapon, no matter how unfair.

His expression hardened. His eyes had that queer glittery
look of rising anger.

"You've just got to claw at me, haven't you, Karen?"

She retreated a step from those brilliant dark eyes.

"Yes, I have! And you know why."

He grasped her under both elbows, pulling her to him and
shaking her like a rag doll.

"*I* know why, but *you* know nothing, you crazy little cat. I
don't know why I bother with you."

His anger only fanned the bright blaze in her.

"Oh, you arrogant ... arrogant ... *devil*!" Her hot words
were dredged up from the best forgotten past; an echo of humiliation, her mother's strange bitterness.

Without a word Guy turned on his heel and left her, his fac a teak carving.

Karen looked after him, struggling against the urge to run after him, to throw herself into his arms where she longed to be to beg him to forgive her ... to try to understand her ... Her pride and her uncertainty kept her there. Her hand moved to her bruised, pulsing mouth and the tears started to well again.

She moved back into her room and slammed the door, then burst into a frenzy of weeping.

Celia, in her room, was not indulging in the unconstructive extravagance of weeping. She was long past the age to risk suf fering the consequences. She was sitting by her window, an exquisite porcelain figure, but she was already planning .. vengeance!

There was no Christmas spirit after that, for underneath the superficial gaiety and signs of good will ran a current of ten sion. With the exception of Pip, who was enjoying himself im mensely, with far too many expensive presents, the tension was beginning to be felt by everyone in the house.

Celia, with all the little oblique ways only detectable to an other woman, was making it her business to make Karen feel like an outsider, with no legitimate claim to the family ... no real place among them. Eva, after all, had been only a second cousin, and that made Karen practically – nothing!

Karen pretended not to notice. There were always so many people calling at Belle Amber; other branches of the family, old friends and visitors, politicians and celebrities, that she found it easy to avoid over-contact with someone whom she felt in her bones was her mortal enemy.

Celia, her eyes unnaturally bright, never failed to take stock of Karen's whereabouts, though with a certain relief she noticed that the girl stayed close to Rikki and made up a four-some with Liane and Colin. Guy was clearly avoiding the girl, and for a moment Celia felt she could have been mistaken, but her razor-sharp senses were too alerted for there to be any mistake!

After that, as if driven by some strange compulsion, Celia kept Karen under constant surveillance. The deep-driven flaw in her character was surfacing under pressure.

New Year's Eve naturally called for a lavish entertainment. Karen went along to Liane's room shortly before seven that evening. If only she could talk Liane into wearing the wig again! With so many people present, there was bound to be comment, all of it favourable, she felt sure. She would incur Celia's wrath, of course, but she wasn't really frightened. Or was she? A shiver ran down her spine and she knocked over-loud on Liane's door, waiting for the cheerful "Come in!"

Liane was standing in the centre of the room rubbing cream into her elbows. Her negligée was a midsummer night's dream!

"Hello, Karo. What are you wearing?"

"That's *my* question!" Karen sank down on a silk-upholstered love seat.

"*You* tell *me*," Liane said surprisingly, now taking to brushing her short curly hair.

"You actually want me to pick the gown for you?"

"Go ahead!" Liane smiled a curious little smile. Karen got up at once and went to the built-in wardrobe, ruffling through the left-hand side of it which held all the ornate evening dresses.

Liane watched, very erect, with a prim air of anticipation. Karen realised she was taking a very long time about it with such a bewildering array to choose from, but there wasn't really anything she cared for. Perfect for someone, but not for Liane. Then, right at the back, she saw it – perfectly plain, but the superb master cut was unmistakable, even on the hanger. Karen reached for it and ran her hand over the beautiful deep coral brocade. She held it out to Liane, who took it with a snort of amusement.

"Aunt Trish bought this. You and Rikki seem to agree on everything."

"It's beautiful, Lee!" Karen's clear topaz eyes held a determined persuasiveness. "Slip it on and let me see."

Liane obeyed, quite cheerful, even gay about it. It looked even better on, Karen decided, and drew a sigh of mingled pleasure and relief. "You've got a lovely figure, Lee. All you have to remember is to keep your shoulders back. With a little practice you won't even have to remember to do that."

"Yes, ma'am!" Liane laughed, and saluted. "You sound like a forthright old lady."

Karen smiled, not denying it. She had heard her own tone. "I do hope I live to be a forthright old lady. I see nothing wrong in it. Guy told me I'd probably floor everyone with a look or a few words."

Liane was smiling back at her and Karen tacked on deliberately: "Now how about . . ."

Liane held up a warning finger. "Don't say it, my girl!"

"But you'd look sensational."

Liane wasn't yielding. "Enough is enough! That's my motto."

"I hope you remember it," Karen said cryptically. "Well, see you later, Miss Amber."

Liane smiled absently. With Karen gone, she turned back to the mirror. She *did* have a nice figure. Funny how a particular style showed it up. She smoothed her hands over the lovely long line of her hips in blissful satisfaction.

In her own room, Karen dressed for the evening with no such sense of pleasure or anticipation. She wore a beautiful sari-type gown Aunt Patricia had made up for her as a Christmas present. The material was a gorgeous Indian silk, embroidered in gold, that Aunt Trish had picked up in her travels. To complement it, Karen twisted her black hair into the unfamiliar style of a heavy chignon. Her mother's peridot earrings, her only jewellery, swung from her ears and she looked beautiful and quite exotic with her strange tilted eyes.

The young men were rather dazed by her, but she realised

this slowly. In the rare moment she stood with Guy and Liane, Liane laughingly commented on this strange phenomenon. She herself was very much in demand. Guy's eyes on Karen were as deep as the night and twice as unfathomable. Karen thought he wasn't going to answer at all, but at last he said tersely: "Beauty is not without a certain awesome fascination. Karen wouldn't be everyone's cup of tea, I imagine."

Liane bit off a laugh and looked to Guy to explain, but he moved away on the pretext that there were more guests arriving. Liane was, in fact, having the time of her life; except for that fearful Dave Barron, an old friend of Rikki's, she explained, and he had this most infuriating manner! Following Liane's eyes, Karen saw a tall, powerfully built young man with a clever-ugly face and who just could be infuriating. Despite this she said clearly: "I like him."

"You do?" Liane gave an exclamation of incredulity. "But he's impossible. You don't know him. Ever since he won that Rhodes Scholarship! The way he goes on. He's even accused me of being intellectually stunted." She patted Karen's arm, then sauntered off in search of Colin.

Less than a minute later she was waylaid by the same Dave Barron, who announced to a first nonplussed then wildly amused young woman: "Rikki tells me you're determined to dance with me!" Liane went into his arms, laughing in spite of herself. At least he was a veritable giant and she could get the most delicious crick in her neck just looking up at him. Marvellous, that! Liane smiled her transforming smile and to her surprise Dave Barron responded, drawing her closer.

Later in the evening when Karen was asked to play, she saw Celia drift out on to the terrace with Colin. Not for Celia to sit through another woman's monopolising everyone's attention. Karen's eyes moved rather bleakly back over the room and she saw Guy was looking at her. He nodded his head imperceptibly and she began to play.

It wasn't cheerful music. In fact it was Chopin at his most

149

tormented, but that was her mood and there was very little she could do about it. Afterwards her hands fell away from the piano with a strange exhaustion. Her audience, rather moved, demanded more, but she smiled and took Uncle Mark's hand. He bore her off to be introduced to a particular friend, fully prepared, he said, to jostle young Rikki out of taking her in to supper.

Of course she was not to escape Colin. There were more of his exploits just waiting to be told, including the brilliance of his latest television commercial for the firm. Karen had to concede that it *was* good! Colin broke off his monologue to say sharply: "Just look at that big oaf with Liane."

Karen didn't turn her head. "I don't think that would describe him. I understand he's a Rhodes scholar."

"Pfutt!" Colin made an exclamation of disgust. "An egghead! Dime a dozen, all of them, and no good for anything else!"

"Oh well, if you say so, Colin!"

Colin redirected his gaze sharply, but the perfect oval face of his companion was quite bland.

"I don't think Liane likes him," she murmured consolingly, but Liane's merry peal of laughter broke out and spoiled the effect of the statement. Colin hunched his shoulders.

Though she had no liking for him, Karen thought it best to mention to Liane that her fiancé was getting restive, so later on in the evening the two girls went in search of him. Soft colour bloomed in Liane's cheeks, her eyes were gay; she looked happy. They moved out into the crowded terrace, then decided on an impulse to re-enter the house through the library. It was easier that way.

The sky was studded with stars, but there was no moon to welcome in the New Year. Liane was the first to see them. They were standing a little way out into the garden, almost directly outside the dimly lit library. Celia was caught in a beam of dull gold, smiling faintly, her silver-gilt head tilted, far back, her

ms slid, oh so gently, possessively, around Colin's neck.
olin's brown head was bent to her, the muscles at the back of
s neck knotted, his back tense, unable to withstand her.

Karen's heart quivered with shock. She grasped for Liane's
y hand, but Liane was gone. She moved with incredible speed;
speed that Karen could neither match nor credit. She herself
ood rooted to the ground, risking discovery. A total apathy
wards life was working its way through her, making her
and limp like a rag doll. Celia and Colin! Was there no man
immune to her?

Colin spun, alerted, and saw her. Shame, self-contempt, de-
ance, flashed across his good-looking face. Celia's voice was
tle more than a hiss: "So – the little sneak-thief!"

Karen didn't answer, feeling submerged by a wave of sheer
chaustion. It threatened to rise up and engulf her on the spot.
he stood fighting it off, until a hard protective shell closed
out her.

"I wouldn't have chosen to see you for the world," she said
a completely dead tone.

"You'll not tell Liane?" Colin looked over at her, completely
anquished. Karen felt a sudden hostility for him that showed
her face. He saw it, mumbled something and even withdrew
s arm from Celia.

"You may as well go," Celia said scornfully. "I can't stand
ou, if you must know. You're your father all over again. Be-
des, you've seen nothing out of the ordinary. Colin is a man
other men are."

"Don't ask me to believe that," Karen flashed back con-
mptuously. Celia stared back at her, loathing in her vivid blue
es.

"*Any* man is my man if I want it that way!" Her silvery
ad was flung up imperiously. Karen would have laughed if
elia hadn't been in such deadly earnest. She took an involun-
ry step backwards.

"You're disgusting!" she said quietly. "A desire for conquest should have some decent limits." She was aware of her clenched hands, the blood roaring in her ears, then she fled before the naked violence in the other woman's eyes.

The New Year pealed in as Karen ran in search of Liane. She found her in her room, lying face down on the bed. Her white, tearless face reflected more completely than anything else her utter annihilation. Karen went to stand beside her and spoke her name. How could she comfort her? With what words?

"Liane!" The girl slipped out of her grasp and went to stand at the window. "Happy New Year," she said tragically.

"Liane dear," Karen's own voice was strained, "you know the strangest things happen at New Year parties. People get thrown a little off balance, do things they would never normally dream of doing."

Liane laughed bitterly.

"Please, Liane," Karen persisted, "everyone downstairs is going a little mad at the moment. It's just an old custom."

Liane actually laughed if the sound was not quite so heart-breaking. "So that's what we saw! Or rather what we didn't quite see. An old custom! Just as well we missed the rest of it. I don't think I'd recover in a whole lifetime."

"Couldn't you be taking this a little too seriously?" Karen found herself saying, wondering at the same time why she was being so inane, but Lee's white face was frightening her.

"Would *you* be caught kissing someone else's fiancé?" Liane asked with bitter derision.

"Oh, heavens, Lee!" Karen tried to be objective, feeling more like crying. "It could happen. One mad moment . . . None of us is perfect. If I loved him . . ." she raved on distractedly.

"And you think Mother loves Colin?" Liane turned on her vehemently.

"I can't imagine how anyone loves him," Karen was stung into truth.

"*I* loved him," Liane pointed out quietly. "Not now. But Mother loves no one. I could forgive her a little if her heart was

152

involved. But Mother loves no one. Her preoccupation with herself is appalling." She repeated herself with dreadful clarity, for the first time in her life facing up to the hard cold fact.

Karen's eyes slipped compassionately over the white, drained face. "You're not coming down again?"

"No. I haven't got that kind of guts. Make up some story for me, Karo. But keep Mother away from me."

Karen hesitated at the door. "She ... neither of them ... realised you were there."

Liane's head shot up. "You never told them?"

"No!"

"Thank you, Karen," Liane said tiredly, and shut her eyes on the world.

CHAPTER X

INEVITABLY the morning followed the night before, and no one with the exception of Guy got up before lunch. One day was pretty much like another to Guy and he always had business to attend to. He retired to his study and didn't emerge. The New Year dinner was scheduled for the evening and no one felt much inclined towards eating before then.

Uncle Mark had a tray in his room and the rest of them drifted in, one by one, to the solarium for coffee and perhaps a sandwich. Amazingly Celia had condescended to join them, and only Karen knew it was not condescension on Celia's part but her warning antennae.

They all seemed to wait for Liane. She slipped into the room quietly, except for her pronounced pallor – stunning! She wore a tailored black linen pants suit, buttoned and buckled in gold, with taupe stripes on the jacket, and a taupe and black silk scarf held her glossy mane. It was Liane at her best, Karen decided, with her lovely lean hips and long, long legs. Celia could never get away with trousers, she was built too close to the ground. Karen sat back smiling.

Rikki, however, let out a long-drawn whistle and even Pip, young as he was, looked his admiration. Karen's instincts told her to sit perfectly still and not say anything. Everyone waited for the bomb to go off, but Celia said nothing! She stirred a sugar substitute into her coffee and said brightly: "We were waiting for you, my darling. I was thinking we might make up a party for this evening and go somewhere exciting. I'll speak to Guy ... when I see him," she trilled. "Why not ring Colin?"

Liane accepted a chicken sandwich from her aunt, then lifted her head blankly. "Who's Colin?" Her aunt maintained an air of desperate composure. Something was wrong, she had felt it. Rikki and Pip were agog, their faces betraying shocked surprise and delight. No one liked Colin.

Celia shot Karen a swift baleful look promising retribution. Karen was shocked by the sudden hardness beneath the sweetly feminine contours of her face. But Celia had admirable control. She only smiled at her daughter.

"All right, dearest," she drawled. "A joke, is it? A lovers' tiff?" The persistent notion occurred to Karen that this was going to develop into an unlovely scene. She turned to her interested young brother.

"If you're finished, Pip, you can go to your room. We might go for a run this afternoon."

Pip looked slightly put out, much loath to leave just when things were developing, but he was used to obeying his sister. He got up without another word.

Celia flashed Karen a look of bright malevolence. "Quite the little mother, aren't you? You're over-attached to that child." Her eyes slewed to her daughter. "Well, what do you say, dearest, or don't you feel up to it?" Her laugh tinkled merrily. "Of course, you'll have to leave that God-awful wig behind."

A pulse beat heavily at the base of Liane's throat. She started to speak, groping for the almost forgotten words, but they emerged with pulverising impact.

"In law, what plea so tainted and corrupt but being seasoned with a gracious voice obscures the show of evil?"

Celia looked genuinely stricken, her face paling into transparency. Even Rikki appeared to be struck dumb. Karen sought Aunt Patricia's eyes. Tension was mounting. There was no telling how far Liane's reaction would take her.

Celia spoke barely above a whisper. "How could you say such a thing to me, your mother, who loves you?" The soft husky voice broke pathetically.

Liane stood up suddenly, a shocking grimness about her mouth. "Pray God no one else loves me in quite the same way!"

Celia let out her breath in a whirring moan. Her eyes flicked venomously towards Karen.

"No, *Celia*," Liane said with great deliberation. "You're barking up the wrong tree. The heart knows its own bitterness. Now if you'll excuse me I do have a few phone calls to make, though it will only take a minute to dispose of Colin." She moved with swift grace out of the room, her head up, her shoulders back, gallant like a young knight.

Celia left them without a word. She was not following her daughter. Patricia Amber stared down into the black dregs in her cup. "What a damnable mess!"

"You do put things very mildly, Trish, old girl," Rikki found his tongue at last.

"It seemed appropriate enough," his aunt replied mildly.

Rikki laughed. "You've got a positive genius for reducing everything to normality, Trish. But then you've been doing it for years, haven't you . . . standing between Celia and us. God, for a minute there I thought I'd have to referee a slanging match. Lee looked as if she was about to up and at 'em!"

"She could hardly attack her mother," his aunt pointed out sadly.

"Oh, I don't know. Think of the times *Lee's* been attacked. You don't always win with a misplaced sense of decency."

Rikki's aquamarine eyes veered to Karen. "There's a story here, sweetie. What is it?"

Karen exchanged a look with the other woman. "Not *my* story, Rikki. This isn't my affair."

"Isn't it now, precious?" Rikki's eyes glinted. "Your coming has changed a lot of things in this house."

His aunt intervened gently, "I think it's about time you demonstrated your ability to suppress your curiosity, Rikki. Whatever Karen knows she's obviously not going to tell you, and for a very good reason, I know."

"Hallellujah!" Rikki jumped to his feet. "This has been a deep spiritual experience for me, girls. You'll have to excuse

e. I've got a little unfinished business myself."

Neither of the two women were sorry to see him go. They ad plenty to talk about!

Whether intentionally or not, Rikki was to complete Celia's ébâcle and contribute to his own sorrows. Much later that eveing when everyone was toying with coffee and liqueurs but ally thinking about Liane's broken engagement and her exaordinary decision to accept Dave Barron's dinner invitation r that evening, Rikki came to the drawing room door, his right eyes elated.

"Kindly step this way, everyone, if you care to be impressed."

Gu looked up with his first smile of that evening.

"Well, I for one would welcome it. Lead the way."

As soon as Guy made a move they all followed with varying egrees of mystification – all except Karen. She knew what ikki had in mind.

The portrait stood on its easel in the centre of the library, laced for correct lighting. The most profound silence fell over ne room, to be broken by Aunt Trish, who said wonderingly:

"Unbelievable!" Her eyes added the words, "And quite eautiful!"

Mark Amber took short quick steps neared the canvas. "My oy, my boy! I never suspected."

"I know," Rikki grinned.

"The first spark, which precedes the breaking out of the reat flame." The quiet voice was almost reverent. "It has a rue musical feeling, my boy. This is indeed our little Karen."

Only Celia and Guy stood back, strangely silent. Karen, as he subject of the painting, was not expected to comment. Rikki vas breaking into quick, uncontrollable smiles, looking from ne to the other. His world suddenly seemed bright and beautiul.

Celia's frown was thoughtful. "It's a highly commendable ffort, dearest. Especially in view of your age." Her tongue moistened her dry lips. "Your subject is over-idealised, perhaps, but that's understandable. But the pose is exaggerated, m' darling. It quite upsets the balance."

Rikki began crowing madly, hopping all over the room holding up one foot. "A blow beneath the belt! Proof, proof I've arrived!"

Celia's eyes flickered spears of resentment. After an age, Karen thought, Guy spoke: "You can put your own price on it."

Rikki just could not conceal his immense gratification. His ardent young face filled with colour. "What more could an artist want...? To be crowned with success during his life-time. Put my own price on it, whacko!" His eyes sparkled impishly. "Perhaps I won't sell to you."

"You'll have to!" Guy said nonchalantly, and moved over to the canvas. "The eyes are remarkable ... the most remarkable feature in a remarkable face. I've never seen eyes remotely like them except for Stephen." He moved slightly, studying the portrait from another angle. "I congratulate you, Rikki. At this rate, you'll surpass the lot of us."

Celia's small gulp of laughter was deprecatory. "Oh, Guy darling, don't be too kind to my poor boy."

"It isn't kind to give someone a false impression of their capabilities," Guy replied mildly. "I think Rikki has great talent, Celia, though why in the name of God he has chosen to hide it all this time I'll never know." He seemed about to say more, then thought better of it.

Karen found herself preparing to face Celia. Every nerve in her body tensed at the knowledge that she must be on her guard. They were all examining the portrait now, admiring it, its loveliness and outstanding technical ability.

"It's gorgeous!" Patricia Amber said happily, her spirits rising rapidly. "Where shall we hang it?"

"Wait until it wins a prize first," Rikki admonished her. "In just over a fortnight!" He leaned over and kissed Karen's cheek. "You blessed damozel! Praise the day Guy brought you back to us." He looked over at Guy, an urchin grin on his face. "How would five hundred dollars strike you?"

Guy raised his head and looked fleetingly at Karen through half-closed lids. "Never undersell yourself, Rikki."

" 'Struth!" Rikki looked as if he would burst into tears! "How about a thousand?"

"I'll write you a cheque," Guy said matter-of-factly.

Karen for one scarcely heard him. Her whole attention was concentrated on Celia, the bright unblinking gaze, that was moving steadily over the portrait. Her heart lunged with a new, secret fear.

On the face of it Liane took her broken engagement extremely well. If she cried herself to sleep some nights there was no one to bear witness to it. Colin's name was never mentioned, for Guy, with the superb ease of chairman of the board of directors, had him transferred to the Sydney office, a piece of information Liane digested with a vast indifference.

To Karen's mind, out of her private heartache, Liane had emerged with a shining new image. Over-long in the nest, she had spread her wings with disconcerting thoroughness. These days Liane Amber was a striking and original young woman, willing and able to think for herself. One evening she announced to the family that she intended working for an arts degree at the University. As Rikki had said, she had been considered a very good student at school. So far as those who loved her were concerned, Liane could have rocketed off to the moon if it would have helped her over a bad patch, but Celia found her daughter's ambition vastly amusing.

"Why, dearest," she said mischievously, "next you'll be joining the women's liberation front and carrying banners."

"My current beau likes intellectual women," Liane said with deliberate carelessness. Her current beau did indeed encourage her to sharpen her wits on him, but he liked quite a few other things beside. Liane looked over to smile at Karen, who shared her confidences, but she gazed past her mother as though she never existed. But Celia couldn't let things lie. She threw back her gleaming pale head and hooted delightfully.

"An *intellectual* woman, what next?" she mocked prettily, her deeply blue eyes skimming her daughter. "Oh well, I suppose ..." It was amazing the meanings Celia seemed able to get into harmless words. She laughed again, her eyes impish. "If a woman has what is really important, she doesn't need anything else. But if she's missed out on that all-important something it might be as well for her to cultivate some of her other resources."

"Her voice was ever soft, gentle and low," Rikki murmured, apparently apropos of nothing. "Do tell us, Celia, what *is* that all-important something?"

Celia's eyes glimmered with secret laughter. One bare white shoulder shrugged nonchalantly. "Why, sex appeal, dearest. I wonder you ask. It's what a man wants."

Rikki took his mother very seriously. "True allure, or sex appeal as you call it, is often a *hidden* dimension, and it doesn't necessarily go hand in hand with physical perfection. If it does, the more powerful the impact, if it doesn't, the impact is still there." His glance veered to Karen. "With a pair of beautiful eyes, it's the expression at the back of the eyes, the reflection of the inner psyche that makes them so deeply alluring ... invested with the timeless fascination of Eve. Where there is only self-reflection, even great beauty palls."

"Gracious!" Celia's small proud head tilted. "I'm grateful I belong in the first category, my darling." Her aimless, drifting eyes returned to her daughter. But Celia's hold on her daughter was broken. Out in the hallway the telephone shrilled and Liane excused herself with an eager light in her luminous dark eyes. "That will be David," she announced, rather breathless for a girl who once professed to find that particular young man "frightful". Celia's eyes watched her daughter's straight back, seemingly unable to accept this newly attained confidence.

Without looking up, Karen could guess at the intent frown that had come between the vivid blue eyes. She had come to realise that there was no adequate explanation for Celia's being the way she was. Being the centre of attention had become a compulsion with her.

The evening dragged on, shadowy and insubstantial. Nothing in this beautiful house was as it seemed. Behind Celia's porcelain face and sweet manner lay a scheming, frivolous mind. Karen paid very little attention to what went on about her, reflecting miserably that Guy was avoiding her.

When Uncle Mark asked her to play she went to the piano with a sense of relief. Aunt Patricia settled herself in her favourite chair to listen, conscious that Karen was disturbed and unhappy. Out of the corner of her eye Karen was watching Guy bend his sculptured dark head to Celia. She was whispering something to him, her lovely face glowing with laughter. Then after a while even Celia was forced into listening because Guy tipped his dark head back and closed his eyes, a faint curious expression on his face.

Karen drifted from one composer to the other ... indifferent now to Celia's watching, waiting eyes. There was nothing to worry about ... nothing to worry about ... nothing to worry about! Yet why was she fighting this incomprehensible feeling?

The next ten minutes gave her the answer. Rikki came to stand in the doorway, incredibly tears in his eyes! His aunt was the first to find her voice, alerted to danger.

"Whatever's wrong, Rikki?"

"What's wrong? What's wrong? I'll show you what's bloody well wrong!" He jerked away, muttering what sounded like basic Anglo-Saxon, but wasn't, then faced them holding a large canvas. Karen's heart stopped beating. She knew what it was. Of course she knew what it was. It seemed she had always known. Rikki turned the canvas towards them and the silence of the grave fell over the room. They all sat motionless, held in thrall. The portrait was ruined, reduced to a dreadful caricature by a childish or wantonly malicious hand! Squiggles of pure pigment were squeezed haphazardly over the sheer topaz of the gown and the face was almost obliterated by the favourite manoeuvre of drawing in a pair of owlish dark glasses. Long curls were added to hang over the shoulders and as a jarring touch of colour – ultramarine beads!

If there was anything remotely funny about the changes no one saw it. The expressions were uniform and menace towards the perpetrator was gathering like mists on a mountain top. Rikki sank down on a chair, struggling with his own private devil of bitterness and frustration. His white, drained face revealed the trenchantness of the blow.

Karen got to her feet with a curiously delayed motion, breaking the tableau. She sat down on the arm of Rikki's chair and stroked his hand.

"Rikki! Rikki!" Under her hand Rikki's long fingers twitched in an agony. She sat beyond thinking for a while.

"Where's Philip?" Celia flung up her head, something almost avid in her expression. The expression, so angrily confident, struck at Karen like a blow. She winced at its impact, her eyes flashing. Patricia Amber looked quickly at her, willing her to be silent. She realised now that Celia *hated* the girl. Karen tried to remain calm but the words sprang up unbidden:

"What's Pip got to do with it?" she said tersely, her burden of worry and bewilderment showing on her face. Celia's eyes glittered. One could almost hear the ice cracking. "We'll very soon know, my dear. Isn't it bad enough without having *you* to contend with?" She spoke curtly, all pretence at civility gone.

"*I'll* get Pip," Patricia Amber said quietly, "though I doubt if it's necessary," she added without emphasis.

"Oh, what a black and dirty night!" Rikki burst out, then reverted to stone. His aunt left the room swiftly, thinking that Celia's stratagem was plain. Her courage almost deserted her!

In the living room Karen felt the mood building up in her. Her nervous system was already reacting to Celia's rapid-fire question and its implication. She turned over the tormenting question in her mind, a strange uneasiness possessing her spirit. Children, even the best of them, sometimes did the most unaccountable things, without realising the effects of their actions. But Pip was so intelligent, so careful of property! His own, as well as anyone else's. She sat ensnared in the pointless goading of her thoughts. Mark Amber lay back in his chair, looking over his steepled fingers. His face was saddened. He would have staked his life on young Pip. Such an intelligent lad! The old, wise eyes studied his nephew.

Guy looked inscrutable as ever, a guard on his thoughts. Nothing was revealed. It was the board meeting face Mark Amber was used to, when Guy let the other party make all the first moves.

To Karen, only a few feet away, Guy seemed frighteningly remote. If Pip was responsible, and who else could be, they would have to leave Belle Amber. It would be an intolerable situation.

Patricia was back within minutes holding Pip's hand. He wore a dressing gown over his pyjamas. His dark head was faintly tousled, quickly brushed over on top. His alert young face, conditioned by a childhood of sizing up adult situations, held a maturity far beyond his years. He crossed to his sister, his dark eyes filled with an unchildlike wariness.

"What's up, Karo?"

She found the soft curl that formed around his ear, brushing it back, without finding words. This was her little brother no matter what he had done.

Rikki threw himself up and away, his temper on the ascendant.

"Leave it to me, Karen," Guy said quietly.

"No, please, Guy!" The force of her protest vaguely shocked her.

"I think you will," he inserted deftly. Controlled as his voice was it flicked at her like a whiplash. It brought her back to control and she subsided.

"Come here, Pip," Guy said evenly. The child went to him at once and Guy took him by the shoulders and turned him towards the light. "I'm going to ask you a question for which there is only one possible answer – the truth. You know that, don't you, Pip?"

The small body tensed under his hands, but Pip's eyes were as direct as his sister's.

"Yes, sir!"

Guy came down to Pip's level. "You know Rikki's portrait of Karen, the one he's entering in the competition?"

"Of course!" Pip's head swivelled to Karen, but Guy laid a finger on his chin and turned his head back to him.

"Have you touched it in any way, Pip? Added a few improvements, perhaps?"

Pip flushed scarlet, then quickly paled again. "I most certainly have not! I'm not stupid, Uncle Guy, and it certainly doesn't need improving!" For an instant he looked like a small replica of his sister. The expression more than anything else, Guy thought with one part of his mind, for their looks were totally dissimilar.

"You've seen it, then," he prompted the child gently. From behind him came a gasp of horror. Celia put her hand to her throat as if to alleviate the strangling ache there. Philip glanced towards her chair, sensing some devious and stealthy purpose.

"Yes, I went up to the studio to see if Rikki was there. I wanted him to help me with something. I draw too, you know. I knocked on the door, but there was no answer. I kept it up because sometimes Rikki ignores you, but he'll let you in if you persist long enough. Anyway, I opened the door for a quick peek and I saw the portrait. It was up on the easel. I just said to myself, 'Gee, you look lovely, Karo,' then I came away. I knew Rikki would show it to me when he was ready."

"And you never touched anything?"

"No, Uncle Guy." There was a flash of spirit in Pip's eyes. "I don't tell lies, Uncle Guy. Ask Karen."

"That's all right!" Guy got to his feet, towering over the child. "You can go to bed now, Pip."

"Aren't you going to tell me what's happened? I won't be able to sleep otherwise." The child's eyes on him were grave and searching.

"Yes, I am, Pip. Turn the painting around, please, Karen." She found the strength to do so. The nightmare feeling was receding. Surely Guy's voice held conviction, a wonderful faith in her young brother. Pip's face mirrored a whole world of dismay.

"Oh, Karo, what's happened to it? Just look at those stupid glasses and the beads! Surely you didn't think I'd do it?"

"Of course not, pet." She got up and hugged him to her, ashamed of her bad moments. Guy put a hand on Pip's shoulder.

"Off to bed now, son. I'll straighten things out here."

Pip had scarcely left the room when Celia lashed out in a fury, her voice out of restraint.

"Surely you're not going to place any faith in that child's integrity, Guy? A ten-year-old who freely admits he was the last person to be in the studio!"

Under the dark gaze her voice lost its passion. Guy's eyebrows shot up with hauteur. "I don't think he did admit to that, Celia. Besides, I've had some experience in reading faces, and the child is innocent. You saw yourself how he reacted. He loves his sister. The idea of defacing her portrait was abhorrent to him. He's far too intelligent, anyway. I'm rather ashamed of doubting him."

Celia threw discretion to the winds. "Well, there's no more to be said. I never thought I would see *you* aid and abet the child, Guy. I'm only sorry I'm not in a position to deal with this myself. It's my son who has suffered!" She suddenly swooped towards Rikki, even at that moment avoiding too close contact.

"Oh, Mother, for God's sake!" Rikki reacted strangely, looking for all the world as though he was fighting a battle he did not care to win.

"The boy's cunning enough, I grant you," Celia said tightly. "You could see he was on the alert as soon as he came into the room."

"Children aren't fools, Celia. I fear you've overlooked that." There was a sombre, relentless cast to Guy's features. The level, quietly pitched voice was devastating. Guy turned to Rikki, and missed Celia's shocked, aggrieved expression. "What have you to say, Rick?"

"I'd sooner endure a red-hot poker than put a name to it," Rikki cried frantically.

There was a speculative look to Guy's eyes.

"You know, Rick, there's always a way round a problem if only one can come up with it." He spoke matter-of-factly as though offering an alternative route to a destination. "A man is as strong as his own determination, his will to succeed."

Rikki stood mute for a minute, his face bleak. "Oh, don't, Guy. I'll go clean off my trolley if I think about it. It's too late. Far, far too late!"

Celia watched the two of them, a waiting stillness in the attitude of her fragile body. A strange emanation of wariness hung about her like a cloud. The origins of intuition are strange! Karen lost colour perceptibly and light flooded the shadows that lurked at the back of her mind. The varying elements blended and shaped themselves into a pattern.

She slumped in her chair, dumbfounded. But didn't defeats demand victories with a jealous nature? Yet what purpose could Celia have in snatching away Rikki's chance at success? But at that moment Celia's reasons didn't matter. Only Rikki mattered, and he was staring at his uncle as though he could feed on that radiant energy that Guy seemed only too willing to lend to him.

Mark Amber struggled out of his chair, drawing the painful scene to a close. "If you'll excuse me, everyone, I'll go up to my room. I suddenly feel old." Without a word Patricia Amber went to him and slipped a hand under his arm. Her eyes as they met Karen's were dark pools of desolation. Her face seemed thinner, drawn. She reached and touched Karen's hand as if for reassurance. A force was on the move that threatened to split up the household; a force she knew she was powerless to meet.

Not so Guy! He stood in the centre of the room and began to quote from Thomas Wolfe, the words and his beautiful voice riveting their attention:

"If a man has a talent and cannot use it, he has failed. If he has a talent and uses only half of it he has partly failed. If he has a talent and learns somehow to use the whole of it he has gloriously succeeded and won a satisfaction few men ever know."

They all stood silently, almost facing each other, and Rikki was looking with piercing intensity into Guy's face. Not one of them was unaffected. Guy's expression was tranquil, but his dark eyes were lit with many small flames. There was something especially challenging and personal in his next words:

"You have a great talent, Rikki. That Richard would have lived to see it! And you have something your father possessed in abundance – a wonderful resilience of soul. I know you'll come up with something."

Rikki's brilliant aquamarine eyes shimmered with the fiercely repressed tears of a young man.

"Uncle Guy," he said shakily, "if I never say it again in my lifetime, I love and admire you." With that he hurled himself out of the room.

Celia laughed. It was an odd laugh, high-pitched and a little wild. To Karen's ears it was not inappropriate!

CHAPTER XI

SUMMER drifted by and nothing happened to visibly ruffle the surface harmony. The Havilland Prize came and went without an entry from Richard Amber. Though Rikki had confided to Karen he was still very much "a going concern" the two-thousand-dollar prize was awarded to a twenty-six-year-old artist from the neighbouring state of Western Australia. Rikki had worked feverishly on blocking and repainting the portrait of Karen, but as he confessed with a white and bitter face, the "face of the vandal" came between him and his work.

To this, Karen thought it better to make no answer. Some things had to remain forever unspoken. A few weeks later, when she read of the approaching Statton-Logan Gift, the rich national award for the most original oil painting, Rikki did not appear to have any interest. The competition was open, he explained, unlike the Havilland Prize, and that meant the finest artists in the country would be competing for the prize. "I'm good, but not *that* good!" he dismissed it with a shrug. If Guy had implied that Rikki hadn't begun to tap his resources Rikki had forgotten about it. Karen said no more, but she was inexpressibly saddened.

Pip returned to school as brown as a berry from long hours under a hot sun, and Karen drove him there and picked him up afterwards, at least until the weather got cooler. In any case, Pip announced to an indulgent Aunt Patricia, by then he could do with a bonzer new bike, like the one Jeff Sweeney got for Christmas.

Celia's behaviour towards Karen was a masterpiece of insolence, but if Karen detected the scorn and the mockery she made no sign of it, treatment which Celia found very disconcerting. With an awareness of Karen's quick temper she had thought to provoke the girl into unbecoming behaviour in front of the family, but Karen was learning. One thing at least, she thought with irony, it was never dull with Celia in the house, and she could still, with some part of her, admire the way Celia used her natural graces with such precise and calculated effect, even to placing cushions for Uncle Mark after dinner. But her own sex was a race apart!

Of Guy, Karen found herself making a continual mental circuit. She was bewildered and more than a little frightened of the strength of her love for him. Love! – the word just slipped into her mind. She had never before given a name to it. It had always been "feeling" or "attraction", anything but what it was ... love! He had only to walk into a room for her heart to turn over; she had only to answer the telephone and unexpectedly hear his beautiful voice to know the full extent of her bondage.

But now they were rarely alone together. Guy saw to that. With his experience of women he was more than aware of her "schoolgirl crush" on him, she thought with a *frisson* of humiliation. By now he would be bitterly regretting the indiscretion of kissing her. Only very young girls took such things seriously. If Guy had married every woman he had kissed, she reflected unhappily, even the vineyards wouldn't accommodate the resultant harem at one sitting.

Liane, at least, was profiting from *her* experience. She was dating Dave Barron quite frequently now, and often Karen and Rikki made up a foursome for dinner or a party or Liane's beloved ballet. They were all of an age, if not similar interests (Dave hated ballet), but they did have similar high spirits. The shared outings went wonderfully well.

One thing alone would have endeared Dave to Karen and Rikki – his ability to bring out the best in Liane, to encourage her to develop her capabilities, to infuse her with new confidence. Dave had only met Celia the once and the meeting had not been successful. Intuitively Dave recognised Celia's hidden

169

"vice" and his manner towards her had been that of a well-brought-up young man in the presence of a venerable dowager. Celia had deeply resented it, but the rest of the family breathed a sigh of relief. Colin had never been popular. "Given enough rope, I just knew he would hang himself," Rikki would comment, trying to draw Karen's confidence, but she never would tell him. Even had she Liane's permission, she couldn't bring herself to further blacken Rikki's image of his mother.

As the time of the vintage drew near a subtle anxiety pervaded the atmosphere. There was always the possibility of a late summer thunderstorm bringing the dreaded hail to ruin the crop. So far everything had gone so well – too well perhaps, to a superstitious vigneron. The berries hung plump on the vine with a soft purplish bloom on them, filled out with the occasional summer shower, and the summer sunlight had been hot but not so hot as to affect quality. It should be a great year, but as Uncle Mark pointed out pessimistically, top wines had been made in quite poor years and now and again, *but not at Belle Amber*, inferior wines had been made in very good years. Fascinating as the fermentation process might be, it was by no means the most important. At Belle Amber the growth of the grape was treated as all-important.

Towards the end of February, sample bunches of grapes were brought in from different parts of the vineyard, for grapes on one vine could be noticeably different from those on another. The berries were crushed and the sugar content measured, then a big conference went on between the family and their technical manager. Now was the time for the vigneron to turn into a chemist. Now was the time for him to display the excellence of his judgment, for on the measurement of the sugar and acid content was based his decision to pick. If the grapes were too high in sugar it would be at the expense of the acids and if the grapes were too low in sugar content the vigneron could not get sufficient alcohol into his wine.

So every day they waited. It was for Guy to give the final

decision, for the gift was born in him and developed to an outstanding degree. He had a recognised palate and a very clear view of the style the home vineyard had developed. The Belle Amber reds were renowned for their superb berry bouquet and their soft and elegant roundness of flavour. There was a deep soft depth of colour to the wine and an outstanding balance of acidity and tannin finish. The vineyard showed two styles, both excellent, but the straight Cabernet had that extra something that lifted a wine into greatness.

So every day they waited. The grapes had to be *exactly* ripe for picking. It was an anxious time, but not for Karen and Pip. They found it wonderfully exciting. This was their first vintage since their return to Belle Amber and nothing could dim its magic.

Each morning it got harder and harder for Karen to get Pip off to school. He even went so far as to stage a very sick "turn" with all the symptoms of peritonitis until Guy promised he would be given plenty of warning of the day of the picking. Pip could stay home from school on that day, and not only that, he could help bring in the crop. There was always room for a small boy on a harvester.

It seemed to Karen, on her endless excursions around the vineyard and cellar, that everyone on the estate was engaged in a welter of conference and comment on this occasion of marvellous complexity – the vintage. Only the foothills, from the first mother-of-pearl wash of the morning to the pink and gold glory of sunset, were the *silent* watchers.

CHAPTER XII

THE day began with a rosy dawn and soon the sun woke her. Karen kicked the sheets aside with a feeling of luxury and abandon, then reached for her lemon batiste peignoir and thrust her arms into it. It was a beautiful morning, one of those mornings almost anything could happen. A great pinky gold sea-horse was trailing his curly tail across the sky and she went to the window and pushed back the shutters the better to see it. She stood poised, her dark head tilted to the sky, polished like a blackbird's wing. She looked ready for flight, young and transient, her tilted eyes oddly beautiful. This was the day, she just knew it!

"Dare I intrude on this pretty scene?"

Karen looked down, startled, to where the feathery Japanese maples were bowing on a wave of silver. Guy was looking up at her, one hand holding a branch back, his black eyes brilliant with mockery. "I did come to wake you in the traditional manner, a shower of pebbles at the window, but I see you've beaten me to it. You look like the dawn bird – do you know it?"

The face she showed to him was full of animation, so different from her aloofness of late. The scented earth was stirring, alive with anticipation and high above them a silver dart of a bird was warbling in ecstasy. She released her breath on a long, sweet sigh.

"What is it?" she whispered.

Guy smiled, deliberately tantalising. "Get dressed and come on down, or I could at a pinch come up." He looked quite serious and Karen took one look at the trailing branches of a creeper and said quickly,

"I'll come running!"

His smile was lazy. " That's what I like to hear. Five

minutes, no more. Those creepers would hold me."

She smiled and withdrew her dark head, moving swiftly. She brushed her teeth, splashed icy cold water over her face; the eyes that looked back at her from the wall mirror were sparkling with all the joy of the morning. She ran a comb through her hair, decided she dared not risk taking time off to apply a little make-up and paid little attention to her choice of a frock – a filamel print in an oriental pattern.

Guy was waiting for her. He tilted her face to him, his dark eyes amused and admiring.

"Oh, to be nineteen and not fear the morning! You look like a Balinese dancing girl. Even the curve of your hair is elegant."

She was unable to suppress the sombre excitement that sprang to her eyes. There could be no escape from Guy. It was so beautiful out there with him, so silent and secret, she could only marvel at its completeness. The scent of the garden came into her lungs and tell-tale colour mounted beneath her ivory skin.

His own eyes held a question. "I hope you don't look at all men as you're looking at me?"

A pulse drummed away in her throat. "I've never *seen* anyone who looks like you," she answered quickly, and evaded him, running on down the path to where the tall poplars soared to the shimmering heavens.

She had to give herself time to control the overwhelming feelings that the sight of him and the touch of him aroused in her. She ran on ahead, feeling the cooling, calming breeze in her face. It whipped her dress around her slender young body and caught at her long black hair, trailing it after her.

Guy caught her up easily and grasped a long coil of her hair. Her lovely mouth quivered and her eyes were starry, dancing with comprehension.

"Why are you forever running away from me?" he asked, his black brows slanting.

"You don't really want to know that, do you?" She looked

173

up at him and blinked rapidly. He didn't answer, but stood there smiling, then he took her hand, ignoring her first, convulsive withdrawal. Lean strong fingers twined through her own and then they were walking, and it seemed a tremendous thing that they should be together, suspended between the sky, filled with scudding white clouds, and the earth with its luxuriant vines.

But she would not meet his eyes, though she knew she had waited for this to happen, through all the days of her life. Her shining dark head was bent and she walked in silence beside this man she knew in her heart was her completion; for without him she would die.

The whole beautiful scene opened out for her in all its dimensions of depth and colour and brilliance so that it almost seemed to her as if she had never truly seen it before. The foothills were bathed in a translucent light and everything was so fresh and strange and beautiful. She could feel the young, eager blood racing in her and Guy stopped on a sunny plateau and turned her about his hands, holding her shoulders, pointing down the slopes. She rested against him, sheafed in the sound of his dark velvet voice.

"I have set my green and clustered vines to robe it round. Far now behind me lies the golden ground . . ."

"Of Belle Amber," she finished softly, feeling a great rush of love for this place. "Lydian and Phrygian couldn't have been more beautiful!"

He smiled. "You've been doing your homework, my lamb."

She turned and faced him. "One never knows when one might be required to quote the *Bacchae* at six-thirty in the morning."

His dark eyes changed expression and he looked out over her head. She tried to recapture his interest, conscious of his sudden withdrawal.

"When the Queen of Sheba came visiting Solomon she brought with her the fruit of the vine."

He laughed out loud, his white teeth flashing. "That would have been the very least of it, I should think!"

She shaded her eyes against the delicate brilliance of the early morning sunlight.

"Don't women start everything now," Guy continued conversationally, "even to the wine cult? It's a very old legend that one of the ladies in the harem of King Jemisheed of Persia was distracted by the pain of headache and drank some of the fermented juice of grapes left in a pot, hoping it was poison. The wine overpowered her and she fell asleep. She awakened refreshed with all trace of her headache gone. Needless to say King Jemisheed and all the court took to this wonderful new pastime."

Karen smiled and Guy turned away and twisted a ripe purple cluster of Sauvignon berries from its wine, holding it out to her.

"Now is your moment to enjoy one of nature's greatest gifts, little one. Crush the berries in your mouth and savour the flavour. The fresh skin of the ripe berry will yield all the character of developing wine. Sometimes it even takes years for a red to regain the floral character of the ripe grape. Try it for yourself."

Karen took the small cluster from him, eager for the experiment. The juice pricked her taste buds and ran down her throat with its special astringent flavour. She swallowed the skin and pips in her first *ampelographical* experience. Guy was watching her, half amused, half indulgent, his dark eyes never leaving her face. Laughingly she tossed the stems away and brushed her fingers against her skirt, the juice still glistening on her mouth, full and enticing.

She looked up at Guy, still laughing, and stopped. The same sensation was stirring in her now as then ... the same never-to-be-borne excitement. She closed her eyes and swayed towards him and Guy took her mouth and tasted – wine. When at last she could speak, her voice was pulsing unsteadily.

"Why do you do it?" All her youth and uncertainty was in her eyes.

He seemed to regard her very gravely for a minute then suddenly shrugged and smiled:

"You've typed me so completely as a villain, my love, I guess I'm just keeping in style. Don't villains always have their way with a woman, and you *are* very beautiful." Her topaz eyes sparkled and her mouth half opened, but Guy laid a warning finger across it.

"No backchat, my angel! That tongue of yours will land you in serious trouble. Besides, your mouth is redolent of violets. Today we start picking!"

Belle Amber was pulsing with life and swarms of itinerant workers moved over the estate, stripping the laden vines. Harvesters brought the grapes in from the vineyards to the winery where they were shovelled into the crushers with a loud *bang bang*. The crushers broke the skins, separating the stalks, and sending the juice into the great thousand-gallon fermenting vats. Fermentation usually took five to six days and there was no one on the whole estate immune to the fascination of seeing the vigorous, bubbling liquid, no more than escaping carbon dioxide.

When fermentation was complete, the new wine would be taken to the wine-press, to separate the liquid must from the *marc* – the skins, pips and stalks. From the press the wine would be run into casks of French Nevers oak, then pumped from its first cask into another, leaving behind the lees that would settle at the bottom. This process would be completed several times before the wine was ready to be bottled – at Belle Amber, usually around its second birthday.

The reds, fermented with their skins, took colour, strength and flavour from them, unlike the whites of Amberleigh, which parted from their skins before fermentation, were more delicate and required much more careful handling. Last year's vintage had produced the two styles: the Shiraz Cabernet, a luscious full-bodied ruby red, and the straight Sauvignon Cabernet, dryer, more delicate, with its exquisite floral bouquet. This year the family and the whole staff were hoping for even better!

That first day was exhausting and the nape of her neck was sunburnt. Karen had no trouble at all getting Pip off to bed. He was out on his feet after a day of unaccustomed toil and excitement. Just to complete things Uncle Mark had slipped a few dollars into an envelope which Karen typed Pip's name on and went off to sleep with his very first wages under his pillow. In no time at all, he told Karen complacently, he would have that new bike with "all the extras".

The house was very quiet that evening. Guy had a late afternoon business appointment and wasn't expected back until late that night. Incredibly, Liane and Rikki had summoned up enough energy to go on to a party which Karen found she could not for the life of her manage. She was deliciously tired out, not at all an unpleasant sensation, but parties were definitely out!

Not long after the two of them left, Karen wandered into the living room and sat down at the piano – nothing energetic tonight, but the sweet nostalgia of Noel Coward. Aunt Trish would be down soon. She was resting a while after dinner, having done every bit as much work as any of the hired help on the estate. Soon Karen became engrossed in working out a new arrangement of the old favourite – "I'll See You Again". She experimented with chords, filling in the time. It was so quiet and peaceful, and *so* prophetic!

A voice from the doorway startled her very completely.

"Girl at a piano! How delightful. Don't you ever get tired of that thing?"

Karen looked over to where Celia, in a swirling pattern of blue and lilac chiffon, stood in the doorway. She was trailing a long matching stole and she looked lovely and quite dangerous.

"Oh, hello! I didn't know you were home." Karen forced herself to be courteous.

Celia, aware of it, gave a brittle laugh and advanced into the room. "I always take off at the vintage. It's so damned boring with tiresome people swarming all over the place. So wearing having to smile at them. Your home isn't your home any more." She waved a small jewelled hand in widening circles in the air and it came to Karen's mind that Celia was very slightly drunk – a most unusual state of affairs, for Celia rarely touched alcohol in any form. She believed it disastrous for the skin and the figure.

Karen shut the lid of the piano, conscious of Celia's active dislike.

"Don't go," Celia said persuasively. "I want to have a little chat with you." She arranged herself artfully in a bergère and tipped her fair head back. "How long have you been here, my dear?"

"Six months," Karen said quietly. There was a kind of sickening familiarity about the scene, as though it had all happened before.

"And the *damage* you've done," Celia said quite pleasantly, not allowing her true feelings to flash out of her eyes.

"I don't understand you."

Now the bitterness in Celia's heart showed in her face.

"I don't mean the way you've alienated my children, my dear. No, don't deny it! They go their own way these days with no thought for their mother. Liane will have me a laughing stock yet with all that gear she goes in for. I'm talking about someone far more important." She sat there almost impassively, a porcelain figure, with a heart like ice. It was foreshadowed in her glittering eyes. "Just let me look at you, my dear. Yes, I can see what he sees in you. Young face, young body, all the beautiful clothes he's bought you. Tell me, my dear, what did you give him in return?" She laughed, delicately, crudely.

Karen recoiled in disgust. "You must be drunk! I can't listen to you."

"You'll listen!" The sweet voice became strident. "Sit down!"

The harshness died out of her voice. "When I was your age I never thought I'd be thirty. Then one day I was thirty. I didn't feel any different. I didn't look any different. But I *was* different. I was thirty – beginning to lose my desirability, all that is important to a woman like me. Now I'm forty with the ghastly years ahead. God help me, forty! Celia Amber, they say, isn't she a marvel, and long for me to crumble." She swung on Karen with frightening vehemence. "Just how long do you think I can maintain this face . . . this figure? The strain is killing me!"

It was necessary to say something . . . anything. Karen was even caught up into a reluctant sympathy for her.

"Please don't upset yourself, Celia."

There was a bitter, dangerous light in Celia's eyes. "Mrs. Amber to you, dear. Once Mrs. Amber always Mrs. Amber."

She got up and found a cigarette from the Chinese box letting the smoke trail like incense to the ceiling. She swayed a little and sat down quickly, her face whitening. "I've had a ghastly, ruinous evening."

Karen made a desperate attempt to avert a scene.

"It's sad, I know, but time is against every woman. We're all in the same boat. One day I hope to renew myself through my children . . . my grandchildren. When I was a little girl my father used to say to me: the greatest unhappiness in life, my darling, comes from reaching for the moon. I've never forgotten it."

Celia's wild crack of laughter was totally unexpected.

"Stephen! My God, that's rich! Reach for the moon? I should say so! He did it for long enough." One look at Karen's shocked look of incomprehension and Celia found her way to a little revenge. She was eager now to placate her *humiliated* ego.

"Don't look so shocked, my dear. Stephen, your father, we're talking about. A terribly sexy man, Stephen, you're a lot like him, worse luck, and Stephen was a good man too, except for one trivial detail; he was on with Trish for years. Dear sainted Trish, the perfect sister-in-law. And Eva never knew! Can you beat it? Imperious, jealous, possessive Eva, *never knew*. A first class affair right under that stuffy nose of hers and she never knew. It was too good to resist."

Karen reeled with a sudden wave of nausea. Everything became clear to her, reflected in Celia's burning eyes, the delicate colourless face. Now she could see behind her father's fatal flight, the dark mystery in the depths of Aunt Patricia's eyes, her mother's bitterness towards the Ambers! But Eva *did know* and someone had told her.

"It was you, wasn't it?" she said sombrely, her own judge and jury, and Celia was convicted.

Celia didn't even bother to deny it but smiled steadily in a most peculiar way.

"You know, my dear, I don't feel the least bit of animosity towards you now. You look so comically tragic. And why not? You've grown very fond of Trish, haven't you? But you can't stay now. You'll have to leave this house, won't you? You couldn't possibly stay on in the same house as your mother's usurper ... your father's lover ... condoning her."

"There's always been something *sinister* about you, Celia, but I never guessed at the full extent of your viciousness. You leave me no way out. You must leave this house." Patricia Amber stood watching them with one hand to her throbbing temple, white to the lips.

Celia laughed – not a pretty laugh. "I'm sure I don't know what you're talking about, Trish. Leave this house? It's Guy's house, remember, and I'm sure he would have something to say about that. Even if you were game enough to try and push me out. You've always had it in for me, haven't you, dear. Don't think I wasn't aware of it behind the stiff upper lip and the gracious civility." She rested her silver-gilt head, looking suddenly drained.

"You're ill. Why don't you go to your room?" her sister-in-law said with forced calm.

Karen gazed mutely across the room at this woman who had

meant so much to her father. Then a strange thing happened to her. She found she didn't care. Her father had loved this woman. That was his affair. Besides, she loved her herself. They could never have been deliberately cruel to her mother. Her head was pounding and the voices were getting fainter and fainter.

Patricia crossed to her side, her voice sharp with anxiety: "Karen!"

"I'm all right." Karen sat down quickly.

Celia looked at them and laughed. "She's all right, Trish. Don't worry about her. You're a thwarted mother and no mistake." She pursed her soft mouth. "So you deny it?"

"I'm simply not discussing it. Not with you, Celia." Patricia spoke tiredly.

"That's no answer at all!"

The other woman seemed to hesitate for a minute, then her eyes found Karen's. "I'm grieved you should hear it this way. I would have told you myself if I thought the old stories would come up again. Yes, Karen, I loved your father, very deeply. It was the strongest, deepest emotion I've ever felt. There was no one before Stephen and it's been my lot that I've never cared for anyone after him. We met just a week before the wedding. How ironic that I should come back from Europe to be your mother's bridesmaid! Our love just happened and it grew and grew, the deep joy in one another's company. We loved, but we were never lovers – I swear this is true. Eva was my cousin, she trusted me implicitly. There were you children. The situation was impossible. We agreed, Stephen and Guy and I, that I should join my mother in California for an indefinite period. That night of the party I know *now* what happened. Eva became inflamed with jealousy. She was stung into saying things that could never be forgotten by any of us. Your father took her home, quickly, quietly."

Her voice broke as she stared down the corridor of the years. "There was the accident, and it *was* an accident, I'm certain of

that. Stephen would never, never have deserted you childre
He loved you far too much for that." She turned back to Celi
"But you didn't tell it that way, did you, Celia? Not to Ev
Not to her daughter. What was it, Celia? Some dark, unco
trollable force, a desire to wound anybody, everybody who w
living. Richard had just been killed. You were so frantic."

Celia looked strange. "Do you know, I think I will go
my room. You always did bore me, Trish. Extraordinary ho
the daughter condones your offence. Like father, like daughte
so they say." She swayed past them, but as she got near Kare
she suddenly spat the words out: "Don't let's go after the san
thing, darling!"

Karen shivered visibly – not at the words but the underlyin
threat of violence.

"You're mad!" she said clearly. "No ordinary woman wi
satisfy Guy, I know that, and you're no ordinary woman – b
he deserves a real woman with a heart and mind, not a painte
frivolous doll with an ugly streak a mile wide."

Celia gave a dreadful cry, which was what it was – a wa
cry! She reached for a small bronze sculpture of mother an
child and hurled it with superhuman ferocity but a woman
poor aim. It missed its intended victim and crashed into an e
quisite Mei Lei vase, shattering it irreparably.

Patricia advanced on her, her tall form menacing.

"Get out!"

Celia trailed her stole, her aberration forgotten. "Don
threaten me, Trish. You're wasting your time. There's only or
person I take any notice of, and we all know who *that* is. A
for this insufferable little bitch, I'll speak to Guy as soon as I
gets home. No one has ever dared to speak to me as she's don
She'll live to regret it!"

They waited until Celia had left the room, then automati
ally the two women fell to picking up the shattered pieces
the once priceless antique. Patricia looked across at Kare
shocked at her extreme pallor.

"My dear, please don't do any more. This has been too much for you. You're as white as a ghost!"

Karen shrugged off her shock and her white face. "I'm not very bright, am I, Aunt Trish? I never knew!"

The older woman made a gesture of complete and utter distress. "Oh, Karen, my child, how *could* you know? I could count on one hand the number of people who did know. Ours was no flamboyant affair, flying in the face of society. My love for your father was deep and enduring, but not to be. Much as we wished it different, the price of happiness came too high."

"Yes, I think I see, but *she*'s quite dreadful, isn't she?" Karen spoke the words baldly. She got to her feet and held out her hand to the older woman. Patricia took the long, slender fingers and gave them a reassuring shake.

"Yes, Celia is dreadful, and perhaps it's our own fault. All of us in some way have conspired to cloak her sins. She's not aware of them and we won't even confess them to one another. Have any of us openly accused her of what she did to Rikki . . . Liane? No, we're all too distressed and embarrassed by her treachery, her lack of love and pride in her own children. But this time she's gone too far!" A blinding migraine was beginning to stagger her eyes, disturbing her vision. She moaned softly. "I'll have to slip up to my room for a while, dear. I haven't had a migraine in God knows how long. Come up with me now. Watch a little television if you can. We'll just have to hide out until Guy comes home. He's never failed me, but there's no winning with Celia. She hasn't even heard of the rules, let alone how to abide by them."

They walked together up the stairway. In her room, Patricia swallowed two largish white tablets and lay down on her bed. Her face in repose was oddly sad. This time Celia had gone too far. She meant to hurt Karen, and that she would never allow! The girl was very dear to her, not only because she was Stephen's daughter and so very like him, but because of her own generous, spirited nature. Celia had made too many people

183

suffer. Patricia closed her eyes. limits." She was aware of her

Hours later, when Guy returned home, it was Celia who got to him first. Seeing the lights of the car sweep up the drive, Karen slipped out of her room, along the corridor, and paused for a moment to look over the top of the balustrade.

Guy was there, standing just inside the front door, the dark splendour on him, his head glossy under the light of the big chandelier. She was reminded forcibly of the first time she had seen him again in Melbourne. Celia stood poised a few feet away from him, furled in a negligée as beautiful and foaming as the sea itself, an exquisite blue-green ... an indescribable colour.

"Guy!" she said in her sweet, husky voice. "I've been waiting for you. For so long! I'm so upset you see."

His dark eyes were alert, his face concerned. "What is it, my dear?"

Celia floated towards him right into his arms, clinging to the lapels of his jacket with pearl-tipped fingers.

"I have to speak to you, Guy. Oh, my dear, I'm so unhappy!" Her silvery head fell forward to rest against the frosted linen of his shirt.

"Celia!" For a dismal moment Karen had the notion Guy meant to kiss her, but he merely put his arm about her frail shoulders. "Come into the library, my dear. We can talk there."

She seemed to melt into him, heartbreakingly small and fragile beside his tall, powerful frame.

A death knell sounded on Karen's hopes. Its reverberations made themselves felt right down to her toes. And now it had become real, her own private nightmare. Was there no escape from human dilemma? *How does she do it?* The words surfaced from the depths of her abysmal disillusionment. *I'll have to go now,* she thought with a kind of dull placidity. The more she considered her situation the more insoluble it seemed. The library door was still shut. Over the house reigned a hushed silence.

Karen wrenched herself out of her trance-like stupor and flew on down the stairs. It was amazing to her how swiftly and steadily she moved. Had she realised it, the tears were coursing down her tragic young face. But she was caught up in an all-consuming hopelessness . . . a monumental despair . . . unnoticing.

Her car stood in the drive. She let herself into it, and her despair disappeared. She felt only resignation and a dull acceptance of defeat. And so Celia defeated everybody as she had done for years. They would have to leave Belle Amber, she and Pip – no doubt with a struggle. Guy would have powerful objections, but she would learn to be a good actress. She would have to accept life in its stark, unromantic inevitability as the women of her family had done to a large degree.

The car slid past the great wrought iron gates. In only a few days – the end of everything! Her mind turned to oddments and through all the confusion, loud and clear, came the memory of Guy's kiss. In the silent portals of her heart she cried aloud: "Guy, Guy, please help me!"

The wind swished through the window as the car gathered speed for the downhill run. With a curious detachment she recognised that she didn't care. Not in the least. Shock carried its own anodyne. She grew sober and contemplative. Not far from here on a fatal night, her father had died. Where had it been? God, that was a bad bend, and she wasn't used to night driving.

Aunt Patricia had said it had been an accident. Had it been an accident? Instinctively she changed down to hold the car on the steep grade. Pip wouldn't thank her for having an accident. What would her small brother do without her? They were a team. Yes, of course it had been an accident, or her mother had grabbed the wheel. With her knowledge of both parents she could picture the scene. The tears sprang into her eyes, blurring her vision. She blinked furiously, wondering what on earth she was doing, out on the road, driving to nowhere ... to no one. She really had no one to turn to.

After a minute she became conscious of lights in her rear vision. There was a car gaining on her. She put her foot down, demanding more speed, but the car in pursuit was by far the more powerful vehicle. It zoomed past her as the road widened with a flash of its long silver bonnet, then pulled up ahead, blocking the road.

This is impossible! Karen thought in an agony, and pulled off the road. She clenched her fists, waiting for that tall figure to loom up into the circle of light. Her unhappiness suddenly broke all barriers, and she buried her face in her hands.

"Karen!" It was Guy's voice as she had never heard it before with anyone. He swung the door of the car open and got in, pulling her to him. At his touch she seemed to go wild, crying and moaning and turning her head away. His hand closed over the tilted curve of her breast, and after the first shock of contact, she held it fiercely to her, letting him feel for himself the tumultuous beating of her heart.

"That's what you do to me," she cried distractedly, past all pretending. "Every time you come near me. Can't you feel it? Go on, feel it, the crazy throb of my heart! Oh, God help me!"

His dark eyes flamed into sensual brilliance. He pulled her across his knees with a tender brutality and that same heart was drumming outside of her, for Guy was kissing her, caressing her, deeply, possessively, as only a man can the beloved woman. A wild elation filled her, transmuting her into one living emotion. Her body became pliant, incredibly soft and seductive, and all through the knowledge that this man really loved her. It couldn't be otherwise. Not this fierce rapture, the exultation, the pulsing, the charging light of the universe!

She clung to him, crying a little at this soaring release, until, exhausted with sweetness, she turned her burning mouth into his throat. Her heavy silken hair fell across his cheek with the clean fragrance of a child's. "Oh, Guy!"

His hand went out and tilted her face to him. "Look at me

186

Karen. Never deny now that you love me."

"How could I?" she said simply. "I always have, ever since
can remember."

Guy took a deep steadying breath. "As soon as I can arrange
, we'll be married. I must have you part of me. I want to be
ble to put out my hand in the night and hear your quiet breath-
ng. I want to be able to hear that breathing changing!" His
and caressed her cheek and she shivered in a kind of ecstasy,
ealising with a little shock that Guy's own hand was trembl-
ng.

"You'll have only one master, my little Karen. I love you —
oo much, my yielding flower." He bent his mouth and found
ers, hearing her speak the one name that hovered like a phan-
om on the edge of her dream world.

"And Celia?"

He drew away from her and looked out to where a late moon,
arge and pale, rose above the vineyards. "Celia is Celia," he
aid slowly. "Beyond my explanations and really, my love, out-
de my sphere of interest. Had Richard lived, she might have
een different. He kept her in hand. These past few years she's
eveloped a certain feeling for me, I know that. Perhaps I re-
aind her of Richard or the what-might-have-been. She was
ery much in love with him and that was the beginning of her
agedy. I've tried to be kind. Some women are strong enough
o get through life alone. Others only live through a man. But
ae woman Celia is, I'd rather not speak of. All that is im-
ortant is, she has never had one indiscreet glance from me.
elia has never been anything more than my brother's widow.
n that alone we've put up with a great deal from her, though
rish has never complained. Sometimes I wish she had." His
and caressed the delicate hollow at the base of her throat. "We
on't be seeing much of her anyway. She knows now that I
aean to marry you."

Karen lifted her head to look at him. "You told her?"

"No, my love. Women like Celia don't need telling." His

187

voice was tinged with a kind of wry amusement. "She'll present no problem, never fear. I guard my own."

He drew her back into his arms, urgently, nuzzling her white neck. "Don't let's talk about Celia."

Six weeks later Rikki was awarded the Statton-Logan Gift for the finest original oil painting of that year. His entry was a portrait, or more accurately an "impression", of his mother. Neither Celia nor any of her friends liked it. It was terribly modernistic and not even recognisably Celia, for it took no account of her exquisite porcelain fragility.

But Karen, when she saw it, recognised it for what it was: a brilliant psychological study. Celia's portrait, unlike Karen's, was never destined to hang at Belle Amber, for by that time, Guy and Karen were married.

A Publishing Event of special interest.

he autobiography of
warm and charming
roman who has
ecome one of the
nost famous authors
f romantic fiction
n the world

The Essie Summers Story

SEE OVERLEAF FOR DETAILS AND ORDER COUPON

The Essie Summers Story

One of the world's most popular and admired authors of romantic fiction, and a special favourite of all Harlequins readers, tells her story.

Essie Summers, the author of such best selling books as "Bride in Flight", "Postscript to Yesterday", "Meet on my Ground" and "The Master of Tawhai" to name just a few, has spent two years bringing the manuscript of her autobiography to its present stage of perfection.

The wit, warmth and wisdom of this fine lady shine, through every page. Her love of family and friends, of New Zealand and Britain, and of life itself is an inspiration throughout the book. Essie Summers captures the essence of a life well lived, and lived to the fullest, in the style of narrative for which she is justly famous.

"The Essie Summers Story", published in paperback, is available at .95 a copy through Harlequin Reader Service, now!

FREE!

*Harlequin
Romance
Catalogue*

Here is a wonderful opportunity to read many of the Harlequin Romances you may have missed.

The HARLEQUIN ROMANCE CATALOGUE lists hundreds of titles which possibly are no longer available at your local bookseller. To receive your copy, just fill out the coupon below, mail it to us, and we'll rush your catalogue to you!

Following this page you'll find a sampling of a few of the Harlequin Romances listed in the catalogue. Should you wish to order any of these immediately, kindly check the titles desired and mail with coupon.

Have You Missed Any of These Harlequin Romances?

All books are 60c. Please use the handy order coupon.

K